FLO MOTION:

A Tale of Betrayal

Imonie Sincere

Copyright © 2015

ISBN: 9780692406106

P.S. Never Give Up Hope Publishing
www.renatahannans.com
contact@renatahannans.com

Cover Designed by D. D'Angelo Green

Dedication

First and foremost, all praises to God Almighty. A special shout out to my mother, Lisa, and my Pops, Titus Sr. To my brothers, Young Pharaoh and Junior, I love you two. My sisters, TyKia and Tigeria, it's nothing but love as well. To my son, Ivan J. Ross, Daddy loves you. To my partner, Saw Money, for making the movement happen. You already know it's LOYALTY to the death of me. To my people who have been loyal since day one: J-BLACK (Orlando's Finest), C-Coop (Tampa Bay Stunna), Julio (Much luv Ock), Rafael (Count Zohar) – I see you, Fresh (Lauderdale 4 Life), Smooth Smith, Hollywood Blow, Nasih, Lil Ronnie (Eastside Duval) and all my partners I forgot, ain't nothing but love. To my beautiful ladies, I salute you and cherish your worth to the utmost. To the soldiers and ladies as well in the struggle, never give up the fight and keep trusting in God.

Peace and Blessings,

Imonie Sincere

A Message from the Author

Time has a very unique way of slowing down, allowing the perfect opportunity for me to catch up with you beautiful readers. My name is Imonie Sincere and I originate from Miami, Florida; however, some of my childhood years were spent in Ft. Lauderdale. Upon graduating high school in the class of 2002, I was fortunate enough to escape the realms of a rough society and attended the prestigious Florida A&M University to further my education.

As a young Virgo, I believe I'm naturally passionate, which is where my love for writing, a desire to bring an exciting vision to the world without using the lens of a camera, stems from. Also, when I read, it brings a rare excitement. My passion is to offer readers the exact same solace. I understand the peace of enjoying a great novel, especially during my temporary incarceration in state prison. This current hardship allowed the intriguing novels by Imonie Sincere to be perfected, just as many tasty delicacies derive from the bitter ocean. The path to success will occasionally present roadblocks, yet to the seekers of entertainment from an intellectual soul; NEVER GIVE UP HOPE!

Chapter 1

The midnight horizon was pitch black as countless stars hung throughout the galaxy while the full cottage cheese colored moon reflected off the white lines, sporadically dividing the lanes of the highway. Paco had the red Porsche Cayenne with 23 inch red alloy rims aired out to the max, doing about 90 miles per hour on Interstate 95 Southbound. Paco was Puerto Rican and Black with a beige-colored skin complexion, complemented by a jet-black, shoulder-length wavy ponytail. He rested his frail 6'2" frame, which was draped in Armani Wear, on peanut butter colored plush leather seats. Eventually, after whipping numerous turns, Paco arrived at his destination—a local strip club in the 305 area code called Black Gold. He glanced in the rearview mirror, rubbing his palm across his hair, smoothing it back, checked his facial features, licked his lip and said, "Let's kill two birds with one stone tonight playboy," all while engaging in a deep chuckle. Walking inside, he made his way to a secluded spot in the V.I.P section and ordered a couple rounds of martinis.

"You want to dance, daddy?" said a slim, curvaceous Caucasian woman wearing an orange thong ensemble, exposing bare cheeks. She stood about 5'8", but the matching leather calf-strapped stilettos added a few extra inches to her demeanor.

"Yes, you can bring that sexy body closer," Paco responded, allowing her to straddle his lap backwards. After a few songs and the nude stripper arousing every fiber of his being, Paco proposed a proposition. "After your shift is done, I'll pay you fifteen grand to join me for a few extracurricular activities tonight." He whispered in her ear.

"Is dis pay cash, Mr. uh...?"

"Paco. Paco is the name and you are Cream, right?"

"Yes, Cash. Rules. Everything. Around. Me. and I am definitely with dat," Cream replied seductively, with an urban swagger.

"If you bring someone, I'll pay you five extra and her ten."

"My girl Rain over there, she's down," Cream stated, pointing towards a voluptuous red bone sistah who was thick in all the right places. Rain had a burgundy sew-in weave that draped down her back with a huge tiger tattooed on her right butt cheek that stood out on her bare body.

"We have a deal," Paco replied.

"Cool. We both get off in an hour."

"Alright, just follow the red Porsche out front. I'll lead us to a nice hotel suite."

"By the way, you paying cash right?" Cream asked again for reassurance.

"Yes, I'll pay you upfront also. I'm just dying to live out my fantasy," Paco said, lying about an encounter he's had on so many prior occasions.

After an hour had passed, Paco headed out the front door, hopped in the SUV and drove off. He peeped in his rearview mirror to see the Lexus truck Cream said would be trailing and stating aloud to himself, "It's official!" Paco led them to a hotel in the Aventura community, checked in to the room, then returned to the ladies' car.

"Come up to room S26 on the fifth floor in five minutes," he was told. Inwardly, Paco had fireworks because once again his cunning scheme worked to perfection like the previous forty seven times in the last year.

"This fake ass Rico Suave better have my money," Rain stated, laughing as the two of them grabbed their bags and headed upstairs. When they made it up into the room, Paco was pouring himself a glass of Hennessy shirtless, exposing his taco meat hairs, while the cash was spread across the bed to solidify his honesty.

"You ladies take your cash and make yourself comfortable. Cream, yours is to the left. Rain, yours is on the right side," Paco stated, grinning wickedly inside.

"Thank you, handsome," said Rain, rubbing on his chest, but silently saying to herself, "Nigga, shave yo chest!"

"How about we all take a dip in the Jacuzzi in the bathroom naked just to get things heated up a bit?" Cream suggested as she removed her clothing.

"Fasho!" exclaimed Rain as she exposed her bare skin and headed to the Jacuzzi. Paco followed behind, offering the girls a few ecstasy pills that they willingly swallowed to crank the fun up a notch. They all sat inside the Jacuzzi fondling each other while smoking a blunt with Paco sandwiched between the two ladies. Eventually, everyone was so buzzed and horny that they made it to the king-sized bed to get extra freaky. The multiple triple stack ecstasy pills that the girls devoured had them so geeked up that they never noticed that Paco wasn't wearing a condom during sex. The ladies pleasured each other while taking turns getting rammed. The entire time, Paco was smiling devilishly because he had two more victims. Now that things were going as planned for the girls, Cream turned the tables.

"Now can we live out our fantasy? Let us tie you up and pleasure that hard monster right there," she stated while stroking his penis with her right hand.

"Alright, my beautiful mamis, let's do it," Paco replied with a Latin accent. Once he was cuffed, Rain flipped the script, brandishing a palm-sized, all-black 9 millimeter silencer pistol, pointing it directly at Paco.

"Now listen, you dummy. Give us the rest of the cash you got, or you're dead," Rain stated angrily.

"Alright, there's fifty thousand dollars in the black duffel bag under the bed. You can have it," Paco said calmly as his penis went limp. All the while, Cream was retracting her steps, clearing any fingerprints that could possibly lead back to them.

"Go ahead. Take the money. You're gonna need it, you scandalous bitches," Paco said while laughing, trying to conceal his fear as the dirty game he'd been playing was now being played on him.

"Why you laughing when you 'bout to get erased, punk?" Rain asked angrily.

"Cause eventually you'll be dead with me. You money-hungry skeezers both been infected wit dat die slow, or in layman's terms, AIDS, bitch," Paco responded, laughing and trying to squirm out of the cuffs.

"You nasty mother..." Cream was stating, unable to finish her statement as Rain ripped four shots into Paco's chest. They grabbed their belongings, along with the cash, then proceeded for an escape through the backside of the hotel, feeling distraught from Paco's dying, taunting words. Despite that, it was now no holds barred on all men. South Florida's nightlife was in for a change and the two women were representatives of a game that would never be played fairly. They embodied death with a voluptuous frame.

Chapter 2

'Another day, another dollar' is the motto that hustlers worldwide live and die by. Everybody wants to get rich quick and if one is lured into the elements of the hustle, which is the streets, it's a must to stay on point. The grimy streets of Miami, located at the bottom of the clip in the 'Gunshine State', is a breeding ground for thoroughbreds and stands for Money. Is. A. Major. Issue.

Draped in hip-hugging Dereon jeans, a tight-fitting wife beater with a pair of baby-blue Air Max 95s, Rain was gliding down 22nd Avenue in an all-black Audi S4 headed towards Opa-Locka. She had just left from altering her appearance, allowing her homegirl Chardonnay at a salon located inside the back of the USA Flea Market on 79th Street to tighten her hairdo up. Rain, now rocking an ebony-colored bob with blonde streaks, had her swagger turned up. Gripping the smooth, black steering wheel with her freshly manicured, powder blue, diamond-encrusted acrylic fingernails, Rain made a left turn on 135th, a one-way street. As Plies' hit song "Get You Wet" ft. Pleasure P played inside the car, she sang along in a very arousing voice that a weak man not bred for the occasion could handle: *"Bet if I suck on dat pussy it will get you wet..."* Rain was just that real.

Despite Paco's shocking news, she never got tested because she came to the conclusion that she would die young anyway. Rain had much hood fame for always being a glamour girl. Her exposing this secret would taint her status and relinquishing her tiara as one of the reigning ghetto queens is something that she refused to do. Swerving into one of Opa-Locka's most infested drug areas known as the Back Blues, which is a hustler's paradise one minute and hell on earth the next when jump-out boys come through, caused Rain to grip her pistol a bit tighter.

In 90-degree, scorching hot Summer heat, crack fiends were sporting windbreakers and jeans with shoes so worn down they were barely visible due to constant walking, chasing that next high.

"Come outside bae," Rain stated over her Blackberry cell. While waiting in the car for her boo to come out, she respected the young dope boys dressed in white T-shirts, camouflage cargo shorts and white classic flat bottom Reeboks with bandanas tied around their heads. They had the block moving like a digital clock getting paid, and even though a few were in their late teens, the streets certified them as cold-blooded killers. Just as Rain was lighting up a wine-flavored Black & Mild, Shaun hopped in the passenger seat.

Chapter 4

Many beautiful women strutted naked throughout the local Miami strip club located on 79th Street called Take One. Hustlers from all areas throughout South Florida came out to vibe and support the naked hustle, making it rain with what they considered loose change, varying from five stacks or better. The aroma of weed and tobacco products filled the air as music was blaring through the sound system with many bad bitches popping and shaking ass for cash. Youngin' sat near the back left side of the booty club, pouring Patron from the bottle into a clear cup filled with ice, simultaneously chasing each sip with a gulp from the Heineken bottle. He was in chill mode, remaining incognito wearing a white V-neck T-shirt, some creased khaki Dickies pants, a pair of white Air Force Ones, a red Miami Heat New Era fitted cap and a matching red G-Shock wristwatch.

Youngin' was never one to be too flashy, despite the minor wealth he acquired from years of hustling and saving. He was being entertained at the moment by a slim, thick brown skin chick who resembled a naked Foxy Brown in her prime. Coming towards the stage from the rear of the club was a thick redbone broad who changed the jukebox to her song selection before stepping into the limelight. She did a quick wipe down of the pole to sanitize and instantly became the main attraction. She was seducing onlookers with every step she took in the all-white leather strap six-inch stiletto heels. Her caramel skin was covered in an easy-to-get-out-of all white leather bikini birthday suit. Her white, cat eye contact lenses were very alluring, and if anyone stared into her eyes, money would simply flow out of pockets because she had the ability to make one feel as if they were all she wanted.

Youngin's attention was focused on the stage as he slouched back in the lounge seat smoking a Backwood, oblivious to Cream approaching. She whispered in his ear, snapping him out of the dazed moment.

"You want a dance, daddy?" Hurricane Chris and Mike Jones' "Drop and Gimme 50" was permeating the aura of the club as Rain was representing her attribute properly as eyes and dollars continued to rain on her at center stage.

"Cream, you good baby?" Youngin' asked, giving her the extra Backwood joint he had tucked behind his ear because he refused to smoke behind her lips.

Blowing smoke towards the ceiling, Cream stated, "So, I see you diggin' my girl Rain." She smiled and exposed four gold teeth at the bottom, which she recently had done.

trunks and a souvenir South Beach T-shirt with some Old Navy thong flip flops covering his pale feet. He sent his entire staff on vacation for the weekend to spend special time alone with his lady friends. Mr. Swanson, a retired stockbroker from New York City, swindled a couple million dollars dealing with Wall Street throughout numerous years within the occupation. When he cashed out, Mr. Swanson divorced his longtime wife, left her and their two daughters a lump sum of cash, then fled to Coral Gables to chase younger, Black vixens he often fantasized about.

"Hello ladies, come on in," he stated, moving to the side as they entered. Once the door was closed, Mr. Swanson offered his hospitality.

"So would you ladies prefer something to drink?"

"No thanks, we're going to do all the pampering for you. How 'bout a massage for starters?" The taller lady replied, stroking his ego.

"No problem," Mr. Swanson responded excitedly. The three of them went into one of the many rooms within the mini mansion where Mr. Swanson had tanning and massage beds located. Everyone was naked, wrapped in jumbo sized white beach towels. Mr. Swanson was wrapped from the waist down, exposing his wrinkled, saggy, pale 67-year old chest. He sat smoking a fine Cuban cigar, chewing the end of it blowing swirls of smoke occasionally.

"How about you lay down so I can rub you down with some of these exotic oils," stated the taller of the women. Mr. Swanson laid down, prepared to be catered to by the two beautiful ladies. He felt like a European boss. The 5'7" caramel toned mami leaned in to whisper something unknown in his ear. She spit an extra sharp razor out of her mouth to slice his throat, never allowing him the opportunity to beg for his life or defend himself. Meanwhile, the shorter, dark-haired woman had slipped away to work on the safe that was stashed in the basement. She had on black leather gloves, along with a pair of latex underneath and a stethoscope that was normally used for measuring heart rates, but was now being used to listen for a certain tick while attempting to configure the combination.

"Jackpot baby!" she shouted aloud, popping the safe open after a few attempts beforehand. They placed the bundles of currency and precious diamonds inside the empty Gucci duffel bags they arrived with, fooling Mr. Swanson who thought they were overnight bags. The two ladies exited the premises, wearing black shades to further conceal their true appearance in case anyone may have been peeking from their blinds in the area.

"Yeah, we met. How you ladies doin'?" he replied, giving them both a firm but gentle business handshake.

"We cool, just vibin'," Jamilah said.

"Yeah, we vibin' but I wanna see what you 'bout," Shay replied.

"Bruh fire now. We gon' sign him. Plus, we 'bout to get ready to record a track together," Danny Boi chimed in, switching gears into work mode, seeking nothing but a hit. This was his first album, so he was hungry. Youngin' also brought a lot of positive street energy, which the industry always welcomed.

"Wassup ladies?" Lyric asked, walking into the TV room.

"Nothing much, just passin' through," they replied in sync with one another.

"Cool. Ay, I got a few tracks I'm feelin', but y'all come in here and listen for yourself. Both of y'all got natural talent so a hit song is destined to happen," Lyric stated.

Lyric lit up a Backwood stuffed with kush then headed back to the soundboard with a thick, grey smoke trailing with each puff he exhaled. Everyone followed suit, walking into the lab as Lyric had his first track of choice playing at an adequate level of sound. Danny Boi began to freestyle sing, creating a hook that instantly had everyone's head bobbing. Lyric stopped him.

"Go in the booth. I wanna record that," he stated.

Shay and Jamilah were just cooling out, doing the honors of keeping the blunts in rotation. Youngin' was deep in thought and as soon as Danny Boi came out of the booth, he stepped in, keeping the cypher ablaze. Lyric continued to edify the song until the quality sound was perfect. Once he allowed the song to play completely, everyone believed they had a chart-topper, but that was based solely upon opinions and critiques of the public.

"I'mma end this session for now to go get some grub. I wanna slide thru da city and listen to a few radio stations so I'll know what music vibe da streets right now," Lyric said.

"Aight, dats straight. I gotta make a lil run anyway," Youngin' replied.

"You ya own man, so I can't say stay out da streets, but just keep in mind we wanna sign you. As a matter of fact, I'll have the paperwork ready in two days," Lyric advised.

"Ain't no pressure," Youngin' responded.

"Fasho. Well, I'mma holla in a lil bit, but if you ever feel da urge to put somethin' down, call me. This job is a non-stop affair," Lyric stated, exiting the studio as Youngin' followed behind. Moments later, Danny Boi, Shay and Jamilah locked up the studio then rode out in the Range Rover, leaving the rental car parked out front.

Chapter 7

"Girl hurry up and get yourself together. Buddy gon' be here in a little while,"Rain stated, pacing throughout the high rise resort at the Lowe's Hotel. Cream was sitting on the plush royal blue sofa topless sniffing lines of coke frequently, trying to escape the inward turmoil she felt from contracting the virus. Cream wiped the top of her nose, removing any remnants of the powder cocaine possibly caked up in her nostrils while taking a swig of Hennessy, simultaneously rubbing her hard, pink nipples with her thumb and forefinger. Cream was higher than gas prices during the reign of George Bush and horny as hell. In the heat of the moment, she laid spread eagle and began to rub her pussy in a frenzied motion because the lime green silk panties created a warming friction that aroused her.

"Girl, you a freak!" Rain stated coming out of the room, stopping in her tracks, shocked by the show Cream had started.

"You know dis pussy look good," Cream remarked, gyrating her hips and throwing her head back in pleasure.

"Dude gon' be here in an hour, but you do look tasty tho. As a matter of fact, stay like dat," Rain responded, prancing back to the room as her titties and ass bounced slowly within the black bra and G-

String panties. Rain returned, approaching Cream toting a pink, eight-inch dildo. Rain stripped herself bare, then slid the moist panties off Cream, tossing them to the floor. Rain straddled her body, pussy to face, allowing Cream to lick her from the back while returning the favors simultaneously shoving the dildo in and out of her warm vagina. Rain caused Cream to have two orgasms within thirty minutes as she skeeted her juices like a Super Soaker water gun.

"Look, tighten yo ass up and let's get dis money," Rain said, slapping Cream's ass hard, taking control.

"Aight, I'm going to shower right now. You coming?"

"Yeah, I got us some matching sexy outfits and robes laying across da bed so let's hurry up," Rain responded while cleaning the mess they made.

After a quick bird-like shower, the two women arrayed their juicy bodies in leopard print thong bikinis with black sheer robes and appearance-concealing masquerade masks. Only their green cat-like eye contacts complemented by unique orange and black hair wraps were visible.

Rain was chilling at the bar area sipping Hennessy with no ice while rolling dirty at the same time. Cream did the honors of being the immediate hostess as the six foot four, 240 pound, midnight black complexion male in a three-piece grey Steve Harvey suit entered the resort. Cream kissed him gently on the cheek and led him over to the bar, allowing him to pour a stiff cup to loosen up. Undoing his tie, he placed the briefcase on the counter and leaned his head back to swallow a shot of whiskey.

"You ladies look nice. Well, I'm a man of my word so here's ya money," he said, popping open the briefcase, exposing the sixty grand that Cream and Rain would split.

Finally relaxed on the couch, dude now sat wedged between the two, making small talk and telling corny jokes. Rain and Cream deserved a career in acting, the way they forged the phony giggles. Rain was actually laughing at his early 1990s swagger because he wore a Gumby hi-top fade haircut as if he was the coolest thing moving. Sensing that he didn't possess the ability to take control, Cream unzipped his pants and began to lick the top of his dick in circles with her tongue. He was immersed in complete pleasure, so Rain decided to fix him another drink. She crushed three ecstasy pills inside, whipping it so good that the residue was unseen.

"Here you go daddy, you look thirsty," Rain said, catering a shot of his favorite whiskey. Cream momentarily paused with his dick in her jaws, allowing him to quench his thirst.

"I wanna eat yo pussy," he said, pointing towards Rain. She straddled his face while he lay on his back. Dude was so engulfed in licking Rain that he didn't realize Cream was sucking his penis with cocaine, causing a deep bone chilling sensation. Despite being paid in full, the women intended to cause deep humiliation as they filmed the entire session. The three of them had sex like porn stars for nearly four hours until their victim could no longer fight off the feeling of being extremely high from the various drugs that he never realized were in his system. While he was passed out, Cream and Rain changed clothes, got the cash and removed the tape with the intentions to blackmail him. Cream decided to write a note. *Thank you for a good time, but we had to go. See ya!*

"Girl, you think he gon' be alright?" Cream asked as they were leaving the room.

"Fuck dat crooked ass cop! By da time his wife see dis tape, he gon' wish he was dead," Rain stated angrily, intending to ruin as many lives as she could before meeting her fate, even though many of her victims were innocent tricks seeking a quick nut.

Chapter 8

"Damn girl, you smell good!" Youngin' stated.

"Boy dat ain't nothing but that raspberry scented shower gel," Egypt said, smiling as she closed the passenger door of the Range Rover.

Youngin' returned his signature smile, asking "So you locked in with me for today?"

"Yeah, it's whatever. I ain't really got nothing to study for, plus my job gave me the day off."

"Aight, well since we got time lemme stop by my peeps car wash so they can tighten my whip up."

"That's fine. I'm just glad to have free time wit no stress, you feel me," Egypt replied, reclining the seat to her comfort level.

Youngin' arrived at a car wash on 79th Street that his childhood friend owned and operated.

"Where you want me at?" Youngin' asked, sliding the window down so his partner, T-4, knew it was him pulling in.

"Come over here behind the white truck. You next fool," T-4 replied, smiling and showing off his two gold canine teeth.

Youngin' and Egypt exited the car and sat under the tent in the plastic chairs, waiting patiently. T-4 had his dreads pinned up while he was sweating, moving back and forth swiftly to make sure that every customer's car was shined and vacuumed to perfection. Washing cars was T-4's hustle and he took pride in his business.

"Dang bruh, I ain't seen you in a minute. Where you been?" T-4 said, walking to the backside of Youngin's vehicle, holding a bottle of Armor All along with a white buff rag.

"You know, just been ridin' round gettin' it. By da way, dis my lady friend Egypt," Youngin' replied, making a formal introduction.

"What they do Egypt. Ay lemme handle dese customers coming thru. I'mma rap wit y'all in minute," T-4 remarked, stepping away directing cars as they came thru.

Youngin' brought Egypt through the car wash with him with the intention of peeping how she would interact in the hood, which was not her natural element. Despite being on a strip in Miami's inner-city known for prostitution, drug dealing and various ghetto activity, Egypt had a comfortable vibe under Youngin's safety.

Approximately thirty minutes after their arrival, Youngin' paid, as well as tipped his partner, left his new cell number, then pulled out and headed south through the city streets. His next destination was the Palmetto Expressway West.

"You like shopping, right?" Youngin' asked as they came to a halt in a parking space at The Dolphin Mall.

"Hell yeah, who don't?" Egypt exclaimed excitedly. Since enrolling in college courses, Egypt hadn't had any extra funds and just to have the opportunity to have something new gave her renewed energy.

"Dats real, so let's go in here and spread some cash shorty," Youngin' responded. The two strolled the mall for about two hours, arms loaded with bags of various sorts of clothing items as Youngin' mainly loaded up on exclusive jeans and fitted caps. Youngin's main focus was to elevate Egypt's swagger because upon initial sight of her, Youngin' noticed a diamond in the rough. Despite them enjoying the luxury of spending money, they were numb to the fact that were being followed.

"Come try one of dese Shish Kabobs over in da food court," Youngin' said, persuading her to partake in one. On each stick, there was savory grilled shrimp, scallops, tilapia fish, red peppers and bell peppers glazed in a spicy sauce, which was a perfect mouth-watering appetizer.

"So what you studying in college?" Youngin' asked, engaging in conversation as they departed from the mall.

"Business Administration with a minor in Accounting. Ya girl is definitely 'bout paper.'"

"Dats real," Youngin' replied, admiring her ambition while reaching towards the control panel to crank the air conditioner notch to level two. Lil Wayne's Carter 3 album was playing a moderate frequency as Youngin' brought his T-Mobile iPhone to his right ear while gripping the steering wheel with his left hand.

"You got a crowd over there?" Youngin' asked, pausing for a second and waiting for a response while glancing into his rearview mirrors. Youngin' noticed an all-white Ford Taurus trailing a few cars back that seemed to be switching lanes every time he did.

"Aight, I'll be there," Youngin' concluded, ending the call. Never one to fold under pressure, Youngin' kept his cool without releasing the slightest hint to his passenger that he felt they were being followed. Youngin' began to accelerate, slightly dipping lane to lane in an attempt to lose his would-be followers. By the time he drove through the toll booth and merged on Interstate 95 North, his black Range Rover was out of sight, out of mind.

At a location down the street from C'est Si Bon restaurant on West Dixie Highway in North Miami, Youngin' arrived at a three bedroom house that was converted into a hair and nail salon. Youngin's auntie operated everything with her two daughters and his Uncle Riley, her husband, was an expert nail extraordinaire. Youngin' led the way inside, greeting as well as introducing his people while his Uncle Riley prepared to do Egypt's nails according to her desire.

"I'm 'bout to step outside for a second," Youngin' remarked, assuring Egypt that he wasn't leaving and that she could relax around his family. Youngin' chuckled to himself while watching them as they resembled a hustling Asian family. They were great at their crafts. While standing at the front puffing on a Black & Mild cigar, Youngin' observed the children running through the streets enjoying life without a care in the world when the sudden vibration in the back pocket of his Evisu denim jean shorts shook him out of his daze.

"Yeah!" Youngin' yelled in an irritated manner.

"You maneuver thru traffic like a champ. Lost me quick," the caller stated, followed by a devilish chuckle.

"Stay off my fuckin' trail befo' I shoot first and ask questions later," Youngin' spat angrily.

"Easy cowboy. I'm just showing you that you can be touched so have my money tomorrow."

"Just be at da spot!" Youngin' hung up immediately. "Laugh now, but die later pussy boy!" he said aloud to himself.

Two hours later, Egypt was in the driver seat while Youngin' rested his Air Force Ones on the dashboard.

"You wanna come vibe wit me in the studio for a lil bit?" Youngin' asked while counting loose money stacks on his lap.

"It don't matter boo," Egypt replied. The opportunity to sit high in the Range Rover gave Egypt a confident, new money swag that was always buried within, but just being around Youngin' gave her swag an outlet.

"Fasho. We gon' grab something to eat of your choice then freshen up first," Youngin' concluded as Egypt couldn't wait to take a shower and pop a few tags on the designer fits, especially the variety of under garments she had to choose from. A pair of panties made from the finer fabrics caused women to embrace the power their pussy withheld.

Chapter 9

"Just go thru da spot. I'mma have my lil homie dem tighten you up," Youngin' stated, hanging up his cell.

Youngin' was standing within the confines of the recording booth with the headphones propped just above his ears. He reluctantly answered his phone after the tenth time the same caller rang his number, only because it became a nuisance to his flow in the booth.

"Crank dat beat up bruh," Youngin' requested, cuing Lyric while pushing his black Dolce & Gabbana hater blocker shades to his face, resting the frame on the brim of his nose. Danny Boi was seated next to Lyric in front of the soundboard while Egypt sat listening attentively, sipping a glass of cranberry mixed with vodka. She was totally impressed by Youngin's talent and ambition, but most of all his refined swagger.

After a two-hour session and four newly recorded songs, Youngin' decided to end the session, choosing not to have Egypt cramped in the studio much longer. He dapped Lyric and Danny Boi and exited his place of business. Instead of settling for being couch potatoes, Youngin' made a suggestion.

"Let's slide out to da Hard Rock Casino and make back some of da bread we chunked earlicr. Plus, we can get our drank on ya dig."

Chapter 10

Cream picked up Rain soon after she spent a grand for an ounce of coke with the 21-year old hustler that Youngin' was preparing to pass the torch to in a matter of weeks. The candy pink two-door Lexus GS 400 on chrome 22-inch rims illuminated the streets as the mozzarella cheese colored half moon brightened the midnight horizon in like resemblance. Within the car behind tinted windows, both ladies resembled the moon, halfway there and high in the sky from tooting cocaine up their nostrils. Eventually, by God's grace, they made their way to the grind for the evening, Club Rolexx. Since they were well-known strippers, they had an all-access pass that allowed them to hustle in different clubs, but not without a fee attached.

They remained outside the club in the parked car for a while, scheming on future victims and taking small shots of Hennessy, preparing their minds to deal with the female vultures present. The ladies sashayed through the front entrance with navy blue designer Prada duffel bags dangling from their shoulders. Despite being juiced up on powder and slightly tipsy, they felt right at home amidst many high and horny patrons popping rubber bands carefree. Only upon walking through the door to the women's locker room did they feel the heat from the envious stares of many naked women pursuing their dream of being hood rich. The women were not jealous as far as physical attributes because they were all top-notch broads; it was all about the bread.

"Girl I ain't studdin' dese hoes. Let's just do what we do," Rain stated, sitting in a chair removing an array of exotic outfits from her duffel bag.

"You already know I stay on dat tunnel vision vibe," Cream replied.

Rain came out of the back with an electrifying presence, wearing a gold with red trim leather black thong ensemble that tied up on the sides, and was easy to come off if necessary. Cream wasn't too far behind, seductively draped in multi-colored fishnet attire. The ambiance within Rolexx this particular night was as any other, with men and women alike lusting for the fattest booty. For the naked hustlers, their mindset was that of a shark trying to survive in a pool; eat or get ate.

Occupying a couple tables on the right side of the club was an entourage of six surrounded by a thick grey smoke, along with numerous bottles of the Ace of Spades champagne as a way of celebrating one of their comrade's freedom. They didn't wear any flashy jewelry, but Rain being a bloodhound for ballers knew the aroma of Federal Reserve Notes very well. She seductively made her way towards them like an experienced money-getter, luring them in with her tight, smooth amazon ass.

Never asking them if they wanted a dance, Rain began doing a move that few have perfected, giving the Jamaican crew a round of applause with her ass cheeks. They grabbed their crotches, loving the performances. The floor that Rain was maneuvering on resembled a seaweed infested oceanfront due to the bills being tossed. Cream also joined her girl, entertaining the posse with a few of her special moves. Many other ladies soon made their way to the area, just like hyenas that flock around food they didn't work for.

"Mi wanna suck on dat phat poosi tonight!" the smooth, chocolate Rasta stated as Rain straddled him with her bare breasts nearly in his mouth.

"I'll do you something better. Mi bring you another punany to lick too. Just tell me where to come," Rain replied in an irritated patois accent, grinding hard to Rihanna's hit single, 'Rude Boy'.

Approximately thirty minutes later, the slender Jamaican dude exited the premises with his entourage, leaving precise directions for Rain to locate him. Upon informing Cream of their after-hour plans, the two paid their dues, freshened up and promptly exited the club.

"Let's go head and get this nigga money, which should be fun too 'cause he got a big dick," Rain stated, rolling up a dutchmaster as they were leaving the parking lot in the Pepto-Bismol colored Lexus.

"I'm a bad bitch and they don't call me Cream for no reason, so let's get it. Plus, I could use a good thug fuck," she said, giggling devilishly.

Chapter 11

"Babygirl, I gotta go take care of somethin' but I'll be back in a few. You welcome to stay as long as you want."

Sleeping in an appealing peach-colored, laced boy-short ensemble, Egypt opened her eyes to attempt to comprehend what Youngin' was speaking about.

"It's six-thirty in da morning. Why you up so early?"

"I gotta make a run, but I'mma leave you da keys to da Rover with a spare house key on there. If you go anywhere, just lock up, but I shouldn't be too long," Youngin' replied, standing to his feet dressed in a white T-Shirt, some grey Enyce cotton sweatpants and a pair of red and grey Nike Air Max.

"Aight, before you leave set the alarm clock for 10:30 so I don't sleep too late."

"Aight boo," Youngin' said, pulling the black and grey quilt over Egypt's naked body.

Youngin' was momentarily intrigued by her beautiful facial features, despite being awakened from a peaceful rest.

Upon exiting the gated Miami Lakes community, Youngin' made a brief pit stop at a self-storage in North Miami Beach. Within the storage facility, he kept fancy furniture that hc never intended to use; it only camouflaged the two chest-high metal electronic safes housing portions of his hustling money over the years. Although he was a major player at the age of twenty-seven throughout the South Florida streets, Youngin' never fancied himself with too many expensive things because he understood the value of saving chips. He possessed two cars and a bachelor's safe haven with plenty of money stashed, which made him content.

Once he left the storage facility, Youngin' drove around cautiously to be certain that he wasn't being followed. After riding around for forty-five minutes like a true veteran D-Boy in a calm state of paranoia mode, Youngin' finally swerved into the parking garage in front of Dillard's at the Adventura Mall. He spotted the silver Cadillac STS on the third floor, but Youngin' continued driving up to the fifth floor, blending in with the rest of the parked cars of the early morning shoppers. Youngin' removed himself from the vehicle, allowing the forest green Jansport bookbag to hang freely off his right shoulder while trekking down the stairs towards the third floor.

"Wassup, you gon' let me in?" Youngin' asked, yanking on the shiny passenger door handle, somewhat startling Mr. Brown. This guy was the lieutenant of the Dade County Narcotics Task Force and crooked as hell. Now at the age of 45, Mr. Brown had been around for a while, extorting major drug dealers. He informed them of the various raids and they paid the cost.

Shaking out of his daze, Mr. Brown unlocked the door. "Hello my friend," he said with a mischievous smirk on his countenance.

Staring directly into the eyes of the six-foot-four, two-hundred-forty-pound Black man wearing a brown blazer, Youngin' replied with a very stern demeanor. "Friends we will never be! I'm here to drop off and pick up vital information. Never forget dat!"

"Whatever, tough guy. You got my money?"

"Yeah, you got dat info? And don't fuck with me either," Youngin' replied, handing over the bookbag stuffed with five bundles of cash totaling fifty grand.

"Just tell your peoples to be cool out there because we put informants in the area hot on your trail. The task force wants you because they know that you're the supplier. Only problem is that they can't catch you with your hands dirty. Their, or should I say our objective is to jam up one of your workers and offer them sweet plea deals to take you down."

"Conspiracy, huh?" Youngin' remarked, rubbing his chin.

"Exactly!"

"Damn y'all crackas playin' a dirty game," Youngin' stated.

"Gotta pay the cost to be the boss," Lieutenant Brown replied sarcastically, fanning through the bundles of money with his fingers.

"Fuck all you pigs!" Youngin' spat out heatedly, getting out of the car.

"Same time next month muthafucka, and don't slam my door!" Lieutenant Brown exclaimed.

Once Youngin' made it back to this vehicle, he called up his main street soldier and informed him to round up the others for a meeting immediately. Unable to calm his nerves due to anger, Youngin' used a Bic lighter to fire up a partially smoked Black & Mild cigar. He drove around with his front windows halfway down, allowing the spring breeze to ignite his survival instincts as he contemplated a scheme to dodge the snare the task force was attempting to strategically arrange. Interrupting his thought process was a ringing cellphone in the center console.

"What's hood bruh?" Youngin' asked, answering the call.

"Vibin' like a rap chemist. I been workin' on a few tracks I want you to murda," Lyric responded.

"Aight, I'll be thru in 'bout an hour."

"Dats a bet. I'll holla at you in a few," Lyric concluded.

"Fasho," Youngin' responded, ending the call as the stop light he was waiting at finally turned green.

After maneuvering through the Saturday morning traffic, Youngin' arrived at a paint and body garage; a multiple car garage with a medium sized office that his ex-con father singlehandedly owned and legally operated.

Renowned for repairing minor dents, excelling in paint jobs, interior upholstery and other various custom work, the building's exterior looked rundown, but within were many state-of-the-art tools needed to perform excellent work. Dope boys throughout South Florida adored Pops Paint & Body because the work was top-notch quality.

"Wassup Pops?" Youngin' asked, stepping into the office.

"Just watching an early round tennis match," Pops replied while sipping a bottle of orange juice.

"Who playing, Venus?"

"Yeah. Serena playing later on ESPN2, but I got an appointment coming through," Pops responded.

"Alright, well I ain't gon' be too long. I just need to holla at my lil soldiers real quick," Youngin' stated with anger rising just thinking about the situation.

"It must be serious 'cause you seem troubled."

"Just a little bit fooling wit dese crooked ass cops!"

"Son, you know I done did twelve years fuckin' wit dese same crackas who call theyselves puttin' down on da dope boys back then," Pops responded in an advisory tone.

"Yeah, I know Pops."

"It's best you cut dem off and if it comes down to it, hold court in da streets."

"Dats exactly what I was thinkin'," Youngin' replied, grinning with intentions to possibly kill the cop.

"I'm here if you need me 'cause you know I strongly distrust and hate cops," Pops stated, reading the murder stare in his son's pupils.

Within ten minutes, Youngin's team of young hustlers arrived promptly dressed in white T-Shirts, camouflage cargo shorts, white Nikes of various sorts and red bandanas tied on their heads. The oldest of the set was twenty one and the youngest was nineteen, but everyone was living the life that they represented. The crew was perfectly structured due to Youngin's coaching, and they even created a renowned name for themselves: Block Boyz.

The meeting lasted every bit of thirty minutes as Youngin' called the plays from the huddle.

"If dem crackas snatch you up, keep ya fuckin' mouths shut. I'll get you out! All they really want is a rat in our organization to bring me down," Youngin' stated, pausing and gazing into the eyes of his little homies, searching for any signs of disloyalty. "Don't open up shop for nobody. As a matter of fact, I know a couple unchartered spots in Broward I want y'all to work. Just chill for da moment. I'mma have a few hoes rent a few P.T.'s and help y'all round so da paper don't stop," he continued. Youngin' then glanced at his wrist to check the time before speaking his parting words. "For now, y'all go blow some money shopping. On my face, no pressure ya smell me. Remember, don't serve nobody till I give the okay. Aight?" Everyone nodded in agreement, simultaneously dapping each other, vowing to dodge the strong-arm law.

Chapter 12

"Your postage cost is $23.08 ma'am," the clerk stated, glancing up from the computer. Paying the price to discreetly mail out two identical life-altering DVDs to different destinations, Rachel Daniels also known as Rain exited the postal office. The dark tinted jumbo shades along with a blonde wig concealed her true features under the beaming sun rays early in the afternoon. She slid her denim jean covered bodacious booty upon the soft seats of her Audi and removed the disguise while straightening her natural hair.

"The flame has been ignited," she stated to herself while staring into the rearview mirror. Upon departing from the postal office, Rain maneuvered the black Audi through traffic hurriedly to pick up Cream in an attempt to promptly arrive at an appointment they both dreaded going to. They arrived at the Miami Dade Health Department, exhaling in unison and fighting the urge to buck the testing that was annually done for women. As they rapidly strutted across the asphalt parking lot trying hard not to be noticed, someone very familiar spotted them. From behind tinted windows, Shaun was engaged in a brief conversation with her other lady lover.

"Damn boo, I know dem chicks. Whatever info you can get on dem let me know," Shaun stated.

"Aight, I'll look into it. Remember I get off work at six and please be easy wit my car, bae."

"I will," Shaun replied, leaning over to kiss her girl's cherry-glossed lips.

Long after the passenger door was closed, Shaun watched her sexy girlfriend strut inside the clinic as the pink scrubs gripped her firm booty just right. Unable to resist the urge raging inside her, Shaun waited for Rain and Cream to exit the clinic. Her plan was to embark on an espionage mission in hopes of uncovering vital information. The silver two-door Acura was perfect because neither Cream nor Rain were familiar with the vehicle.

Once they came out of the clinic, Shaun was hot on their trail, maintaining a safe distance of at least five cars being careful not to alert them. Twenty minutes later, Rain dropped Cream back off at the gate of the apartment community in Miami Lakes upon Cream's request because she needed to walk and clear her mind. That was perfect for Shaun because her boredom mixed with curiosity was the driving force that fueled her continued pursuit of Rain. Upon losing sight of her target in traffic, Shaun came to a halt at a red stop light at the intersection of Pines Boulevard and University Drive while her eyes roamed the area, seeking the possible direction Rain may be traveling. Fate had Shaun's number as she spotted her target to the right stepping out of the car in the parking lot of IHOP restaurant approaching a yellow Lamborghini. Shaun kept her eyes fixated on Rain until she noticed the tall Jamaican dude embracing her into a tight hug, followed by a lip-locking kiss.

"Oh hell naw!" Shaun stated angrily with her jaws dropped in amazement, never bothering to park properly and stopping directly behind the yellow Lamborghini. She grabbed her chrome .22 handgun out of the Prada Baguette purse she toted, stashed it in the small of her back and then jumped out the car.

"Damn, you can't take ya girl home?" Shaun stated, approaching the two, kissing the Jamaican dude on the cheek.

"Mi girl, you didn't wanna ride wit di badman when mi was down ya ere," the Jamaican dude stated, stepping to survey his ex-main lady.

"I did until you sized me and let dat otha bitch come visit you. By da way, I took care of dat problem tho," Shaun said smirking.

Inwardly, the Jamaican dude knew that the monster in Shaun he helped create had killed the gal because he hadn't seen or heard from her in two years.

"Baybee you crazy dere but wa gwon?" he asked. Shaun was about to respond, but Rain cut in.

"Wassup is me. She is old news and I'm fresher den baby powder." She stepped to his side and grabbed his arm.

"Rain, if you know like I do, you betta get yo stupid ass somewhere!" Shaun stated in a threatening tone as dude stood shocked by the fact that the women knew each other.

"Shaun, bitch I knew you wasn't shit!" Rain responded in an agitated manner. "As a matter of fact, you can have dis tired ass dick 'cause me and Cream done trained him already anyway," she continued. As she spoke her last comment, Shaun punched her in the nose, knocking her to the ground as the blood dripped. Shaun kicked Rain hard in the gut then leaned down over her, pulling the .22 out and raising it to her face.

"Stupid bitch, I should blow your brains out right now." She noticed the patrons inside the restaurant staring out the windows. Shaun got up and sprinted towards the car. "Follow me. We need to talk," she stated as the Jamaican dude was fleeing the scene himself. Once Shaun crossed County Line Road returning to Dade County city limits, she detoured off to the Carol Mart parking lot in hopes that her ex-lover would follow, and he did.

"You crazy dere girl you know," he said while his Lamborghini door was up and he was positioned in the seat sideways with a black glock resting atop his lap. Shaun stood between his legs.

"You already know I'm living like dat when it comes to you, but why you ain't tell me they freed you?" she asked.

"Couldn't contact you."

"I was hurt so I foolishly stayed away. Anyway, how you got out?"

"Baybee di Babylonian system can't keep mi dere. Plus, me bredren dem paid a lawyer dat was betta and di appeal he got granted. So dem muthafuckas had to free mi outta dere."

"Damn, Zion, I been fucked up since you left me out here," Shaun stated, thinking about the mediocre lifestyle compared to how they lived prior. She was actually living above average, but before the Feds snatched Zion from the turf, the two of them were living extremely lavish.

"No worry, da king back for redemption ya ere," Zion stated with his heavy patois accent.

In the midst of their conversation, Shaun's phone sounded off with its Plies 'Bust It Baby' ringtone. Zion gripped his pistol, slightly paranoid, paying close attention to his surroundings as cars and people were moving in all directions. Paranoia was a natural reaction to Zion after being locked away for five straight years. When Shaun removed the cellphone from her ear, her countenance was a very shocked demeanor as her bottom jaw was wide open. Coming back to her senses, she stated, "Tell me you didn't fuck dem two hoes."

"Naw, mi twin brudda come here from da island and he was wit 'em. I see da bitch ya ere and sexy I thought so I called and act like him, straight," Zion replied, looking directly in her eyes performing his former ritual that blinded her for years; lying.

"Babe you lucky 'cause her and dat white broad just tested positive for HIV," Shaun responded, shaking her head in disbelief.

"Say, say dere how you know dat?" he asked with his right eyebrow raised. Shaun spent the next five minutes explaining everything in detail.

"Dose sour pussy bumbaclots must die ya ere!" Zion exclaimed as the lines in his forehead scrunched up.

"I'm down to ride, but let ya brother know ASAP so he can get help before it's too late."

"Respect babygirl. Mi gone, but call me so we can handle dat soon ya here."

"You got my word," Shaun replied, hugging him and then heading to her girlfriend's auto. Once Shaun returned to the confines of the automobile, she shouted, "Thank God!" due to the fact that her constant hustle mode never allowed her and Rain to engage in intercourse, despite them vibin' heavy at one point.

Chapter 13

"We gon' try to add two more songs to ya mixtape and begin circulation to get a response form da streets," Lyric remarked, spinning around in the swivel chair.

"Aight, I'll come back tonight and finish up," Youngin' replied, passing a kush-filled blunt.

"Actually, I want you to roll wit me and Danny Boi tonight to da club so we can get a firsthand reaction on how da streets feeling da track you on wit him," Lyric said.

"Aight, I'm 'bout dat."

"I just need to smell out da atmosphere. By da way, in 'bout three months, we gon' ride to Tallahassee fa TJ's DJs. Dat way you'll create national exposure. Dats why this mixtape is important," Lyric stated, puffing the herb and placing his expensive laptop inside the Louis Vuitton bookbag.

"No pressure 'cause da kid ain't scared to chase paper."

"Check it, I'mma come scoop you up so don't worry 'bout driving," Lyric responded while reaching underneath the soundboard, unstrapping the black glock he had concealed that was legally registered.

"Just call me," Youngin' stated, dapping Lyric before dispersing the recording studio. On his way to pick up his business associate, Youngin' made a brief stop at KFC to order a small three-piece chicken box.

"What dey do?" Youngin's passenger stated upon his arrival.

"Whatever I tell 'em. Ride wit me so we can talk. Here, roll up a few," Youngin' stated while sliding his counterpart a Ziploc bag full of dro. They rode and smoked while Youngin' explained how the narcotics task force was setting up the snare. These were drastic times, until the eye of the storm bypassed them.

"I'm going to switch up turf and slide up to Broward, ya smell me. I got a bunch of bricks left that I know only you can handle cooking properly if you down with me. Don't worry, we got anotha spot and you gon' be well taken care of," Youngin' remarked.

"Ain't no pressure, but one question."

"What's dat?"

"What you think these crackas got on us?" Shaun asked.

"Dey got nothing, but dey tryin' to make one of da Block Boyz squeal. That's why I shut down shop."

"That's what it is. Ay how 'bout my ex-ol man, Zion, out here on da streets," Shaun stated, dumping the tobacco from a Backwood into the empty KFC cup, preparing to twist another blunt.

"I thought fool caught a dub in da Feds," Youngin' replied in a shocked manner.

"He did, but he somehow won his appeal. I bumped into him as I followed dis silly stripper hoe, Rain, from da health clinic while dropping my peoples off at work," Shaun responded. She commenced to briefing him on the whole scenario.

"Damn, I'm glad you told me dat 'cause I know dat bitch Cream too," Youngin' said, shaking his dome horizontally in disbelief.

"Ay, pull over into da Jerk Machine real quick for me. I see dat same yellow Lambo parked out front dat Zion was driving when I last seen him. I want you to meet him 'cause he was talking 'bout gettin' back what he lost," Shaun said.

"How you know dats da same whip?" Youngin' asked skeptically.

"Cause I see dat I LOVE JAMAICA license plate," Shaun replied with a smirk. Youngin' began to pull into the parking lot area of the restaurant and instantly shouted.

"Oh hell naw!"

"What's up?" Shaun asked, sitting straight up nervously.

"If dats him I ain't fucking wit him 'cause he an informant!"

"How you know dat?"

"Cause dats da same Cadillac dat crooked ass cop was driving last time we met. When we spoke, he was talking 'bout informants being out here," Youngin' stated while watching Zion walk away from Lieutenant Brown's automobile.

Shaun was watching in shock herself before blurting out, "Dats why dey let his fuck ass out! So he can send otha niggas in. Damn dese snitches gotta pay," she said with hurt in her heart, but subsided it due to her loyalty in this game.

"Don't sweat dat shit 'cause I got a trick fa both dey asses," Youngin' replied, glancing over at Shaun noticing a single tear fall down her cheek, but he never mentioned a word because he knew she was once in love with Zion; He taught her everything she knew about the streets.

Chapter 14

A severe thunderstorm was brewing outside as oversized raindrops fell from the sky and bright blue streaks of lightning permeated the horizon occasionally. Within the interior of the South Beach high-rise condo, Danny Boi was positioned in the midst of two cash counters, wrapping every ten stacks with rubber bands. He was accompanied by Shay and Jamilah, both draped in black bras and matching boy shorts with the words 'Dynamic Duo' in gold embroidery on the ass area. After tallying all the currency, it came out to an even eight hundred thousand each.

"Damn, I love y'all two. Y'all da real muscle behind dis Dynamic Duo E.N.T machine and without y'all it just wouldn't be right," Danny Boi said, leaning back in the wooden chair, lighting a blunt and blowing smoke towards the ceiling.

"We down to ride 'cause we love you daddy," Shay replied, rubbing his chiseled chest as she stood between his legs, giving him an eyeful of pussy due to the stiletto heels boosting her height a few extra inches. Jamilah stood behind the door blushing like a schoolgirl while mixing Long Island Iced Teas for them to drink. In the midst of the arousing bonding session, Danny Boi's phone rang as his brother

Lyric's face illuminated the screen. He tapped Shay's peach-shaped ass while answering the call.

"What we got bruh?"

"Nothin' much, just wanted to inform you dat da album release date gon' be da same week as TJ's DJs. According to how things been happening, I felt deliverin' da release party to da Tallahassee streets would be da perfect homecoming for you," Lyric stated enthusiastically.

"Dats a bet! I'll call a few of da homies and have them pass da word. You know how da city talk," Danny Boi responded, overjoyed.

"I already handled dat lil bruh. I sent two singles off the album via email to da radio station and also paid for radio airtime promotion for the event," Lyric replied.

In the midst of the conversation, Danny Boi noticed Jamilah dancing seductively on the stripper pole mounted in the living room while Danny Boi's album permeated the airwaves. Danny Boi grabbed his nearly erect penis through his denim jeans.

"I'm definitely excited 'bout all dat big bruh! Honestly tho, I got a few things to take care of right now at da crib so I'mma get up wit you lata," Danny Boi responded, amped up now standing holding his dick with his left hand.

"Dats real. I'll holla at you in a lil bit," Lyric responded, laughing and knowing exactly what his brother was up to.

"One hunnid," Danny Boi concluded.

Danny Boi's eyes were filled with lust as he was in motion towards the bar fixating his stare upon the two horny Black goddesses. Once he settled his guts for the occasion, Danny Boi tossed the remainder of strong liquor to the back of his throat, then approached the ladies as an aura of swagger and confidence surrounded his presence. The ladies danced in an arousing manner, as if it were a remake of the 'Tip Drill' music video. Danny Boi gently palmed both women's pussies from behind at the exact same time while they were making their ass clap. He was the only one who had the pleasure of witnessing.

"Ladies, enough of dis striptease. Y'all come to da room and give me dat good pussy," Danny Boi stated after about ten minutes, walking into the room stroking his penis.

"Oooh shit, you make my pussy wet daddy. Please let me suck dat dick," Shay commented, also following to the room.

Chapter 15

"Pops, what you up to?" Youngin' asked, coming through the garage of the paint shop.

Pulling the protective mask off his face, Pops answered, "Just hookin' up one of dese young dude's Chevy."

"Yeah, I see you gettin' money round here, but do you got a minute? I need to holla at you." Instantly, his old man dropped everything and led his son into the air-conditioned office.

"What's on your mind son?"

"Dese streets! I've been signed to a rap label and I wanna leave da streets behind."

"So what's stoppin' you?" Pops asked.

"My loyalty to my lil homies who been helping me eat out here," Youngin' replied with visual signs of stress upon his face.

"So why not bring them up under yo wing, sorta like your very own promotion team."

"I thought about dat but... it's a great idea," Youngin' remarked, having an epiphany. "But da real problem is dis crooked ass narcotics lieutenant dats been extorting me out here."

"Okay, tell me about him," Pops stated.

"Every month I give 'em fifty bands to supply me with information about future busts so I'll be ahead of da game. Only problem is I strongly believe he's setting me up, making me think that da Feds on me when really he's da one sending his informants at my lil homies on da block."

"Go with your first instinct son, because if not you'll regret it. Make your last payment to dis pussy and whatever his name is, cut all ties ASAP!" Pops advised.

"His name Lt. Daniel Brown," Youngin' stated as Pops stood up instantly.

"Hold on, I can't believe dis shit! Is this a huge Black muthafucka possibly in his mid-forties?"

"Yeah, wassup?"

"Son, about twenty years ago I was twenty five at the time running the streets in my respective area and this same dude was copping yayo at least three times a month, spending good. I thought the nigga was a young hustler because this snake was good at what he did. Come to find out, after serving dis dude for nine months, he was actually an undercover. He took the stand, sending me up da road for all those years when you were young," Pops said as Youngin' continued to listen attentively.

"Your uncle searched for this dude for almost six years, but no luck. To think dis shit is a déjà vu moment, but extra personal now because he fuckin' wit blood."

"Pops dats my bad, I should've been told you."

"Naw, it worked out perfectly 'cause now me and your uncle can scratch that itch we been having for all these years," Pops replied in a reassuring tone.

"Dats real Pops, but I never would've thought Unc was livin' like dat 'cause he over dere fuckin' wit dat beauty salon," Youngin' remarked with a slight chuckle.

Pops smirked and replied, "Son, ya bloodline is a bunch of thoroughbreds. But gone head and rest ya nerves. Everything gonna be aight. I'mma get with you later 'cause I need to finish dis jitterbug car."

"Alright Pops, I'll catch you later." As Youngin' was driving away from the car garage, he picked up his phone in an attempt to call Egypt, but was deterred from the thought as his phone rang at the same time.

"What's hood soldier?" Youngin' asked Solo, the lieutenant of the Block Boyz.

"I'm vibin', but at da same time it's been a bad day big homie."

"I'm listenin'."

"Man, swerve round by Bunche Park. I need to holla at you in person," Solo replied.

"Nuff said," Youngin' stated, knowing it was serious, also admiring Solo's street savvy to want to not discuss anything over the phone.

Fifteen minutes later, Youngin' discreetly pulled into the park, spotting his lil homie sitting on the hood of a grey Monte Carlo SS smoking a Newport short cigarette.

"What they do, Lo?" Youngin' asked as he approached him with a handshake.

"Man da fools dem," he said, pausing for a second in disbelief, shaking his head before continuing.

"Shad and Marlo was on pills, weed and liq trippin'. Dem niggas was speeding on da I and lost control, causing the car to flip a couple times, crashed into some cars, then finally smashed into da brick median in da middle to a stop."

"Tell me dem fools ain't dead," Youngin' replied. Solo never said a word, he just brought the fifth of Hennessy to his lips, then poured nearly half the bottle's contents on the ground, confirming what Youngin' dreaded.

"Dats only da half tho," Solo stated with anger in his voice.

"What could be worse?" Youngin' asked.

"Dat dumb ass nigga J.B. locked up!"

"For what?"

"He caught a sales charge. After you said shut down, dis nigga crept out to da block anyway. I couldn't contact fool for like two days. Come to find out dis nigga sittin' in county for serving an informant. Just like you said big homie," Solo stated angrily, lighting another cigarette to calm his nerves.

"He got bail?" Youngin' asked.

"Yeah, but dis nigga ain't solid. I had my lil bust it baby pull da police report since dat shit public records, ya smell me." Youngin' nodded his head in disagreement. "Dis bitch ass nigga got your name all through the black and white as his supplier and boss. I'm contemplating a way to kill da nigga now!"

"I definitely want you to handle dat, but be sure it's clean."

"I'm 'bout payin' a baser to post fool bond, then I'll be there to scoop him up. Da nigga birthday in two days so I'mma have a fit and some drank in da car so he'll have his guards down."

"You, Speed and Will do dat. Once y'all take care of dat, we gonna lay low in Tallahassee for a while. I got dis mixtape we gon' pump too so we ain't gotta be in da streets too heavy. You wit dat?"

"It's whateva big homie 'cause I ain't going in da slammer."

"Aight, give them two da lick. Give all ya shit away except ya clothes and I'mma start y'all off fresh. Whatever you do, don't tell nobody you leaving. I'm banking on your loyalty," Youngin' said in a serious demeanor.

"Bruh, you embraced me when my ol boy and ol girl died so my loyalty to you is all I know. Will and Speed out here thuggin' like I'm thuggin' and we move as a unit, you smell me. Dis Block Boy shit is all we know and you made dat possible. It's death befo' dishonor wit us," Solo responded, reassuring Youngin'.

"Aight den, we in dis shit to win lil homie."

"I got you," Solo stated, dapping him with a shoulder to embrace before they departed.

Chapter 16

"Wassup boo. Why you so uptight?"

"Just got a lot on my mind," Youngin' replied.

"You want to talk about it?" Egypt asked.

"I'm cool babygirl. But anyway how was your day?" Youngin' stated, leaning back on the sofa.

"It's funny you ask because I was just about to tell you that I got accepted to Florida State University's Grad School for the fall semester. I was afraid to tell you 'cause I really wanna be your lady and if I'm there it would be hard," Egypt stated, sitting Indian style with her hands on Youngin's thigh.

"If it's meant to be, a few miles apart won't keep me away," Youngin' replied, thinking to himself, *Man she fallin' fa da kid fast.* "I know bae, so I don't even know why I was worried. Anyway, whatever is going on I got your back regardless," Egypt responded, rubbing her hands up and down his chest.

"Some things, bae, you may never understand about how I live."

"I've heard your raps and I comprehend the truths you speak, so trust I can visualize how you live. I'll never try to change you; only complement you by staying focused on my goals in case you ever need me," Egypt replied, assuring him that she wasn't lame to the streets, despite her being a college girl.

"Damn bae, you down like dat?" Youngin' asked, cracking a smile.

"Most definitely. Now you relax and let me show you how down I am," Egypt concluded, unzipping his shorts and dropping down on both knees between his legs. Egypt pulled his ten-inch dick out the boxer slit, using her moist tongue to lick in circles around the tip. Youngin' leaned his head back in pleasure as she licked and sucked every inch, while massaging his testicles with a warm gentle palm.

"Yeah girl, like dat. Suck daddy dick," Youngin' stated, coaching her through each motion while gripping the back of her head. Egypt could feel Youngin's dick swelling in her mouth as he stated, "Ooh shit, bae, catch dat," shooting a load of semen in her throat as she swallowed it all.

Egypt wiped her mouth. "Ahhh daddy, you taste good."

"Dats all da pineapple I drink," Youngin' stated, removing the remainder of his clothes, except his sneakers.

"That's why it was sweet like dat," Egypt replied, stripping down to her black and red laced lingerie set.

"Ooh, I like dat." Youngin' spoke while stroking his dick. He laid Egypt on the sofa spread eagle as he slid her panties to the side and commenced to licking and sucking on her clit in a movement that few men had mastered. Egypt tried to control her orgasms, but the experienced pussy eater was too much for her to handle, as he also had two fingers jabbing in and out of her pretty pink Brazilian waxed area.

Once Youngin' caused Egypt to shake uncontrollably on three different occasions, he was ready to put the pound game on her. Egypt was now in doggy-style position with her legs dangling off the sofa and her phat ass tooted up towards Youngin'. Youngin' stood tall, placing one foot on the couch for leverage while digging deep inside of her. As he slid her panties to the side, Youngin' gripped them as if he was riding a bronco with one hand and the other hand was positioned on her waistline. Egypt was wetter than the Caribbean Islands during El Niño's raining season.

When he slid inside her walls, Egypt moaned, "Ooh Bay-bee," while bouncing her ass on his dick like a loose rubber band.

Youngin' shifted gears, stroking long and slow in order to gain a nice steady rhythm. Once Egypt became accustomed to the size of Youngin's dick spreading her out, she yelled, "Ooh daddy, get dis pussy. Fuck me harder!" Youngin' shifted gears as he turned Egypt on her side, pounding her long and hard, causing her titties to bounce up and down like a '64 Chevy Impala. The wetness of her gushing pussy was an arousing sound to Youngin's senses as their skin clapped rhythmically with every stroke.

"Ooh baby, I'm cummin' again," Egypt moaned.

"Me too!" Youngin' shouted before pulling his dick out and releasing his load on her chest and face as she smeared it in with her fingers, then licked them seductively. Afterwards, they both showered and fell asleep naked. Egypt rested her head on Youngin's chest while he kept her comfortable with his right arm wrapped around her.

Youngin' was only asleep for a few hours before arising in the wee hours of the night, contemplating his future moves. Not wanting to wake Egypt, he went into the living room to watch sports highlights on ESPN while smoking a blunt, then drifted deep into his thoughts.

Chapter 17

Days later, Youngin' pulled up to a low-key motel located on Pembroke Road in Hollywood, Florida, driving a grey two-door Pontiac Grand Prix rental car. Shaun stood in the doorway of room 222 waving to him as she spotted the car pull up the backside parking lot.

"What's hood baby?" Youngin' asked, stepping through the doorway closing and locking it.

"Just vibin, reporting the work," Shaun replied in a sexy baby-like voice.

"Dats real. Everythang out in da whip. We'll bring it in in a lil bit."

"Dats straight. Well I got dis room to sleep in and 227 to do what we do," Shaun responded.

"Aight bet. But shit run me down da street to Pollo Tropical in your car real quick so I can get somethin' to eat, plus peep da vibe 'round here at da same time," Youngin' stated, rubbing his belly.

"I did an observation before I got da room so we straight, but let's ride tho."

"Fasho," Youngin' replied calmly, always wanting to double check everything. They sat in the car at the parking lot of Pollo Tropical talking while devouring their food before going back to the motel. Youngin' entered room 227 with two roller suitcases along with a blue over-the-shoulder Nike duffel bag. In each of the suitcases was thirty kilos of powder cocaine; the duffel bag contained bundles of cash and a semi-automatic Mac 10. Shaun had all the necessary materials needed to perform her specialty. Youngin' was there to weigh and bag up the drugs, as well as be a designated shooter if the occasion deemed for it.

The blueprint of the room was a basic television, bed, bath, a window A.C., and most importantly a gas stove. At check-in, Shaun gave the older Puerto Rican owner two-thousand dollars. He exchanged the keys, never asking for any personal information due to business being on a drought. They wrapped their face to withstand the stinky aroma and the process they were all too familiar with began. Coking one kilo took a bit under an hour, so their mindset was to camp out for a couple days. The first night, they grinded a full twelve-hour shift, completing the first twenty-seven, thanks to Shaun's ambidextrous ability to work two pots at once. After cleaning the area and stashing everything inside the retractable drywall roof, the two of them exited the room nearly being blinded by the bright orange early morning sunshine.

They went to room 222, showered, then rode out in the Pontiac to Golden Corral for the breakfast buffet. Once they made it back to the room, Shaun rose from a peaceful rest as Youngin' was already awake.

"You ready to get money?" Youngin' asked, turning around from the counter where he positioned the portable DVD player that was showing the movie *Paid in Full*.

"Ya girl feel brand new. Give me a few to freshen up," Shaun replied, smiling while stretching her arms to the ceiling.

"Do ya thang. Ain't no rush; we gon wait til the sun go down anyway," Youngin' stated, refocusing his attention back to the DVD screen. Forty-five minutes later, Shaun exited the bathroom smelling like a fresh bouquet of scented roses, wearing a pair of leopard print laced boy shorts with red trimming and a bra to match. She was drying her hair with the towel and noticed Youngin' staring, grabbing his dick.

"If you want this pussy, come get it," Shaun stated in a teasing demeanor.

"Dat pussy definitely lookin tasty. Just keep me on appointment status. For now, let's handle business... pleasure later," Youngin' responded, fighting his inward urge to fuck Shaun at the moment because she was definitely a badd bitch.

"Yeah you right," Shaun replied, sliding into a pair of black skinny jeans, jumping up and down because her phat bubble booty made them tough to get into. Once Shaun did get into the jeans, they had the painted on illusion. She also draped herself in a tight black wife beater shirt and a pair of all-black Timberland hiking boots.

The sun was setting in the westward horizon as the night clouds were moving in the east. They remained in room 227 and commenced to doing the same as the night prior. Shaun was cheffing the goods to perfection while Youngin' chopped and bagged everything into eighths, quarters, halves and wholes. This night, whether it had been pure adrenaline or just an infatuation for the money, they managed to complete the remaining 33 kilos, finishing the job. Afterwards, they tidied up the entire room, removing everything and placing it in room 222, then fell asleep for a couple hours and set the motel alarm for 5:00 p.m.

Once the alarm clock sounded off, Youngin' rolled over groggily, tapping Shaun's leg to get her up and going. They were rounding third base and in order to make it to home plate safely, it was a must the two of them keep it moving.

"I'mma put everything in your whip since it got tints and you follow me in the rental car."

"Aight, but keep your eyes open," Shaun replied in an advisory tone.

"You know my head stay on a swivel," Youngin' responded, pulling out a bag of ecstasy pills. They both popped two and headed out to the cars, drinking bottled water. Shaun stopped at the desk to return the keys to the older Puerto Rican gentlemen.

"This is for never seeing me here," she said, while peeling off two stacks. He nodded his head in agreement. "And if you find anything in the rooms, get rid of it," Shaun continued while exiting the building.

"Si Señorita," he responded, fanning through the bills as if he had hit the Florida Lottery. Making a smooth journey through the streets, they ended up at Pops Paint & Body garage.

"Pops, everything is in these two suitcases right here," Youngin' stated, pointing towards them, "Don't forget to get the U-Haul truck, load it with furniture and stash this along with the rest of the furniture and dope inside the furniture."

"Son, I'mma take care of that. You must've forgot who the O.G.," Pops responded calmly.

"Yeah you right, Pops."

"Now calm down. The black Navigator is in the garage and it has all the stash spots you need," Pops stated. Even though Pops did paint and body work, he mastered the art of creating stash spots within vehicles, but it was rare that anyone outside his family knew this.

"Thanks, Pops. By the way, this is the lovely lady Shaun I was telling you about."

"Nice to meet you, Shaun," Pops responded, shaking her hand firm, but gently.

"I'm fine."

"That's a given," Pops remarked in a flirtatious manner before continuing. "Before you leave, your unc wants to know when you want to make that other drop off."

"Tell him to be ready in three days," Youngin' responded, sitting in the driver seat of a black Navigator.

"Alright."

Youngin' and Shaun rode out in the SUV smoking a blunt of dro', traveling west towards a location in Miami Lakes. The two of them looked at each other excitedly thinking in accord, *Damn the Gods of the Underworld must be in our favor tonight.* The same yellow Lamborghini that Zion drove seemed to head in the same direction... possibly the exact destination. Youngin' continued to drive as if not seeing Zion, careful not to alert him.

Twenty minutes later, they arrived at the condominium community that Cream live in. Youngin', having been there before, knew exactly where she lived, so he allowed Zion to go through first then followed suit ten minutes later already knowing the access code to the front gate. Shaun sat inside the truck while Youngin' crept around back to cut the wires to the alarm system and disable the service. Youngin', camouflaged with the darkness, watched through a small crevice in the blinds as Cream and Zion took turns snorting lines of cocaine off a glass plate. They got up to move into the bedroom as Youngin' shook his head side to side, amazed at how sexy Cream looked in the royal blue lingerie. He was also in disgust because she was dying slowly.

Youngin' being a jack of all trades also mastered the art of picking locks. Before going in, he crept around the back and signaled Shaun to join him as they both crept in without a sound through the patio door. In the midst of creeping through the house, they could hear various moaning and slurping sounds signifying that Zion and Cream were having sex. The room door was wide open as Shaun and Youngin' approached the threshold with barrels raised. They intruded in the midst of a 69 session with Cream sucking Zion's dick facing the doorway as his face was buried in Cream's ass, never noticing the two figures before him.

"Get yo face out dis AIDS infested ass you pussy ass nigga!" Shaun screamed with two pistols drawn.

Cream stopped bobbing on his dick, looking like a deer in headlights as Zion's head peered around her round white ass cheeks.

"Don't even fucking move or I'mma blow your brains out!" Youngin' threatened, noticing the subtle movement by Zion. Instantly, his dick went limp as Cream was still holding onto it with her left hand.

"What's this all about?" Cream asked, scared as hell.

"First of all, you and dat nasty bitch Rain got dat shit and y'all passing it around not giving a fuck who you kill!" Shaun shouted.

"I, I...." Cream shuttered, but Shaun cut her off and shouted.

"Shut up, bitch!" She slapped her with the butt of the pistol, knocking her to the floor. "And you," Shaun stated, pointing her guns at Zion, "You snitch ass nigga! I can't believe you turned sour on da same streets dat made you. You a piece of shit!" She screamed as Cream lay on the floor holding her face, scared to move.

"You know what, fuck you two muthafuckas. Y'all gon' kill me anyway so yeah you right I took a deal with dem shit-eaters. I'm da original king of dese streets and it's been dat way since I killed ya brother!" Zion spat out, not realizing he just set off a ticking time bomb. Nearly fifteen years ago, Shaun's older brother was murdered when she was a tender twelve year old. It was a drug-related incident and the killer was never apprehended. Reality never dawned on her that during Zion's five-year run, she was aiding the exact person she vowed to kill, had the details ever been uncovered.

"You pussy muthafucka," Shaun shouted, standing over him firing three rounds in his chest and one in the center of his face. Shaun turned and hit Cream twice in the back of the head and once in the back. Her pent-up anger was ignited, but Youngin' shocked her conscious yelling, "Let's go!" They fled the scene the way they came, evading the peeking, nosy neighborhood Crime Watch looking through the windows.

They rode in silence for a while until Youngin' remarked, "You know I'm clearing it to Tally in a few days right?"

"Naw, I was under the impression we was going to Broward, but I'm glad you told me 'cause I gotta find some place to lay low."

"I can use ya help if you down to ride."

Shaun turned with her back to the passenger door facing Youngin'. "Of course I'm down. I don't have any family left and you da only person I trust."

"Dats some real shit, but what about ya girl?" Youngin' asked. "She got a dude comin' from prison in three months so I know dat what we had don't mean shit. Plus my heart is some place else," Shaun stated, exhaling a deep sigh.

"Alright, get your stuff together and don't tell nobody you leavin'. I got a different hustle fa us when we get there too. We still gon' move work, but in da meantime put it on da backburner 'cause money is not a problem fa us right now. Trust, ya boy is definitely strapped."

"I'm down fa whateva," Shaun responded.

Once they retrieved Shaun's car, they traveled to a secluded spot near Opa-Locka airport and poured Kerosene on the vehicle, setting it ablaze in case any witnesses ID'd the vehicle.

Chapter 18

"So you working late again, huh?" Mrs. Brown asked sarcastically, with tears streaming down her smooth cheeks.

"Yeah, babe. I've been handling a very intense operation that's time consuming, but in a matter of days it will be over. I'll make it up, I promise."

"Aight, whatever. I'll see you whenever."

"Damn honey, what's wrong with you?"

"Nothing. Do you," Mrs. Brown exclaimed, hanging up the phone, never allowing him a chance to respond. Mrs. Brown sat frozen in place watching the tape of her husband's fiasco with two women in masquerade masks. She was suspicious of the white girl who had a tattoo on her thigh that she believed was the same one she noticed while performing the duties of the Pap smear test at the clinic she worked at just a week prior. As the tape was nearing the end, her suspicions were confirmed as the white girl strutted to the bar, raising the masquerade mask to drink and revealing her true identity. "This nasty son-of-a-bitch!" she screamed aloud, realizing her husband was HIV positive because she was the doctor who treated both patients that particular day.

At the bottom left corner of the television screen was a date three weeks prior, which caused Mrs. Brown to shout, "Thank you Lord!" She was relieved because for the last five months, her plastic toys were all the pleasure she received, due to her husband's so-called busy work schedule. Mrs. Brown had to literally beg for a good tune-up, but was avoided every time, which she now was thankful for.

Directly in front of the television, Mrs. Brown stripped down out of her scrubs, getting naked in the process, preparing to take a hot shower. In the midst of her relaxed state of mind, she mumbled to herself, "The hell with him; it's time for me to go out and live a little. As a matter of fact, I'm not even coming back."

After her shower, Mrs. Brown packed all of her personal belongings and loaded them into her car. She draped herself in a form-fitting, red mini-dress with an exclusive edition of red and black pumps, complemented by a few accessories. Before exiting the house, she uttered, "What has this bastard been keeping in that safe?" She knew of all his crooked entities as a narcotics cop, but being a good wife she stood beside him regardless, gaining his trust during the 11 year marriage. She had always known the code to the safe, but chose to never invade his privacy… until now.

Inside were bundles of cash that Lieutenant Brown confiscated from various drug dealers, along with a couple pistols that seemed to be fairly new.

Mrs. Brown was a scorned woman, but far from crazy, so she cleared the money out of the safe and left the guns behind, vowing to never return to the place she once called home.

While driving north on the Florida Turnpike, she phoned a reservation at the Hard Rock Casino & Resort, securing one of their many suites for at least a week, charging it to her MasterCard. After arriving at the Casino Resort, checking into the suite and dropping her luggage within, Mrs. Brown ventured around downstairs to sip on margaritas. Eventually, she came to a hall of the main blackjack tables, creating a drink tab while betting casually and allowing her mind to drift away in a state of long awaited serenity. Unbeknownst to her, she was being eye-sexed by a dapper-dressed older gentleman for the last fifteen minutes. Despite being forty-one years old, Mrs. Brown was reminiscent of a very fine wine that preserved its freshness with age.

"Hello gorgeous, how you doing?" the brother who was staring asked, as he approached the blackjack table. Mrs. Brown was briefly mesmerized by the dude's immaculate appearance, and also intrigued by his khaki linen pantsuit, which coordinated with chocolate-colored Stacy Adams shoes.

Spinning around on the barstool, she motioned the dealer to deal in another gambler, simultaneously stating, "Actually I'm enjoying myself, even though my luck hasn't been too great though." She smiled while sipping her drink.

"Maybe I can ignite some good luck."

"Seems to be you already did, 'cause I finally won a hand," Mrs. Brown paused to soak in his swag and continued, "So what's your name handsome?"

"I'm Charles Young, but all my friends call me Pops," he replied, extending his head as a formal greeting. Aroused by his swagger, Mrs. Brown remained humble.

"Pops, huh? Well, my name is Charlene. So who are you here with?" she asked, glancing over his shoulders.

"I'm hanging out with my brother and sister-in-law who is somewhere 'round here. Honestly, I stayed off from them when your beauty grasped my attention." Underneath the dress, her muscles were twitching rapidly due to the smoothness of his voice, along with the alcohol igniting her hormones.

"I'm actually glad you came over because I was a bit lonely and I didn't want this stunning dress to go to waste." Charlene stood posing as she gracefully spoke.

"You're definitely turning heads tonight," Pops replied, licking his lips and admiring her luscious frame.

"Seems to me like you have all the right words to say, playa."

"Actually I'm no playa. I've been single for the last eight years since my wife passed away."

"I'm so sorry to hear that," Charlene replied, as the corners of her eyes began to water when her thoughts were shifted to her trifling husband.

"What's wrong cutie?" Pops asked, noticing the twinkle in her eyes fading. "Just thinking about my husband and his no-good cheating ass. He finally struck out for the last time tonight."

"How about we stroll over to the live jazz club and talk about it over a few drinks."

"Yeah, that's cool 'cause I don't need all these folks in my business anyway," she responded with a slight smile.

"Alright, let's roll," Pops remarked. He wrapped her around the waist and led her to the section of the casino resort where the numerous free twenty-one and over clubs were located. His brother, Riley, noticed the movement, so he tipped his hat to an original player that had not lost a step. Riley wasn't worried about where he was going because they drove separate cars, plus he understood it was finally time for Charles to continue on with life

because he was still handsome at forty-five and his
deceased wife wouldn't want it any other way.

Chapter 19

"Good morning, South Floridians. I'm Melinda Alvarez broadcasting live with Channel 7 News. I'm currently in a very serene Miami Lakes community. The neighbors reported an unusual foul odor coming from the condominium behind me so they alerted authorities. Upon investigation, two decomposing bodies were found; one Black male and one white female; both were naked. The woman has been identified as Cristin Summers, who also answered to the name Cream, as we were informed by a local night club source. The male victim's name is Zion Faison, an ex-drug dealer. Sources also released information about the victim working as a police informant during the time of the murders. Authorities have yet to release any more information pertaining to possible suspects. If you have any information, please call 1-800-CRIMESTOPPERS."

Lieutenant Brown sat frozen in front of the television at home in his private den in total disbelief upon hearing the report. Attempting to drown out his emotion, he began pouring rapid shots of whiskey, the beginning stages of an alcoholic syndrome. Every morning he came home through the garage a little after 5:00 a.m., purposely avoiding his wife, who was out the door at the same time every morning. Once the liquor began to settle on his stomach, Lieutenant Brown headed to the interior of the home to eat a light breakfast. He plopped down on the white sofa in the living room with a plate of bagels and strawberry-flavored cream cheese. He then noticed a pile of clothes on the floor in front of the television, which was still showing a blank, royal blue screen. He said to himself, "Damn, she must have been watching a porno," while pressing play to get a glimpse at what she was viewing.

The figures on the video caught him by surprise as the bagel he was about to bite was dropped to the floor instantly. After witnessing the contents of the tape, he was in awe at what his wife may have seen and wondered how he would escape the drama this time. Never allowed the opportunity to ponder on his lies, Lieutenant Brown's cellphone rang.

"Talk to me," he stated, then listened attentively for a second.

"Alright, I'll be there in an hour," Lieutenant Brown concluded. He trotted upstairs to change his clothes, negating a shower due to the recent bad habits he acquired. While scanning through the closet in search for a nice suit to change into, he noticed that many of the designer suitcases were missing and attempted to call his wife but to no avail, only reaching the voicemail.

"Fuck!" he screamed, angry and frustrated all in one. Whether it was intuition or strictly paranoia, Lieutenant Brown instinctively ran to the safe and rapidly punched in the access code. His biggest fears were confirmed once he opened it. He vowed to personally kill his wife because she made off with 600,000 dollars, leaving a one dollar bill inside just to antagonize him. He sped along the interstate headed to the MDPD headquarters, anticipating the urgent news that he was told awaited him. Before Lieutenant Brown could cross the threshold of the building's entrance, he was greeted by one of his fellow narcotics officers out front.

"Man I don't know what you've gotten yourself into, but it seems to be some very stinky shit," the pale-faced white dude stated while taking a puff from the Marlboro cigarette he was holding.

"What's going on?" Mr. Brown asked nervously.

"I don't know for sure, but I know that Internal Affairs Division is awaiting your arrival."

"Alright, thanks Bill." He nodded his head as the lieutenant adjusted his tie that seemed to get tighter with each step he took, choking out his life slowly.

"Oh by the way, your partner Jamal said give him a call," Bill shouted as Lieutenant Brown was entering the building. Lieutenant Brown gave him the thumbs up as everything seemed to be moving in slow motion while he made the trek to the narcotics department, only to be re-routed to the Internal Affairs Department by the secretary given instructions to relay the message. He walked into the conference room and was greeted by a middle-aged white woman and a frail, average-height Black gentleman wearing wire-rimmed glasses.

"Lieutenant Brown, you have been a very important asset to this force for numerous years, but lately your integrity has come into question," the white woman stated, getting directly to the objective of the meeting.

"Un-huh," Lieutenant Brown hummed.

"We recently received a very gruesome video involving you and two other parties engaging in sexual favors, with you exchanging an undisclosed amount of cash for their services." With that statement, Lieutenant Brown cringed due to embarrassment.

"We believe the footage may have been leaked to the media and therefore, you have been suspended without pay, pending investigation," she stated, never breaking eye contact with him until he dropped his head in disgust of his own actions.

"Before you leave, Mr. Brown, I'm also here to inform you that you are on the brink of a federal indictment. I'm a representative with the DEA and we have reason to believe that you've been aiding and abetting drug dealers, accepting payment in return. You are possibly to be linked to a ring of conspiracy operations. My advice to you is invest in some great lawyers," the Black gentleman stated, closing the brown folder that was before him.

"One more thing… place your badge and gun on the table," the white woman concluded. Mr. Brown exited the MDPD fuming with rage and nothing but vengeance permeating his conscious. He vowed to kill his soon-to-be ex-wife, along with the other woman who recorded the career-shattering video. She was on his top priority list and he knew exactly where to begin searching, the exact same place of their initial acquaintance, the strip club scene.

Chapter 20

"I had my partner who's a well-known DJ host the mixtape for you," Lyric stated.

"Dats a bet. So when you plan to let da streets hear it?" Youngin' asked, pulling a Backwood stuffed with kush from behind his ear.

"That's on you, playboy, 'cause I already got 'bout four boxes filled with CDs in the other room."

"Oh yeah?" Youngin' replied in a humble yet excited tone.

"Yeah and I used the picture of you posted in front of da Rover with all jewels on dat night me, you and Danny Boi went out for your mixtape cover."

"Damn big homie, dat was quick," Youngin' responded.

"You know we 'bout our grind round here. Oh yeah by da way, da girls set up a Myspace and Facebook page in case anyone becomes an instant fan and wants to reach you."

"Man, I don't know 'bout dat cause I'm in da streets for real to ever have time for da internet love."

"Naw it ain't nothin' like that; it's all just to allow you a better networking opportunity to build a fan base and every now and then drop a new track on there for them. We must show the major distribution companies that you are marketable," Lyric replied, puffing the blunt that was passed to him.

"Dats real. At the same time, there's somethin' I need to holla at chu 'bout."

"Talk bruh-bruh, I'm listenin'," Lyric replied attentively. Before Youngin' could say anything, Danny Boi stuck his head in the room.

"Man y'all come check dis out! My video done made it to number five on 106 & Park's countdown in just two weeks!"

They all went into the TV room, never taking their eyes off the flat screen, until the video went off and they were able to gauge the reaction from the studio audience's comments. Everyone was all smiles knowing that Dynamic Duo Entertainment was on the rise.

"Since we all here, I got somethin' I wanna holla at you 'bout. I must keep it real and let y'all know I'm slidin' out of town, possibly to Tallahassee," Youngin' stated.

"Damn bruh, what's up?" Danny Boi asked, concerned about his label-mate, but more importantly his partner.

"Man dese slimy ass police tryin' to tie me into a major drug ring," Youngin' stated, pausing for a second to make sure he had their attention. Noticing that everyone's ears were attentive, Youngin' continued giving them a complete story about the turn of events in his life over the past couple of weeks, negating to speak about the murders that have taken place. "So dats why it's time for a change of environment before dis shit begin to stink, ya dig," Youngin' stated, concluding the brief synopsis.

"Yeah bruh, I feel dat 'cause I had to come down here to get away fa a while, but to be honest I been kinda hood sick so I'm finna go back soon," Danny Boi replied, assuring Youngin' that they understood the circumstances.

"Shit, it actually works out fa da betta 'cause Supastar J Kwik, the DJ who hosted ya mixtape, da hottest thing up there possibly in da country right now. You can get airtime on da radio fa a small fee of course, plus we got a cousin up dat way in da real estate business. She'll get you in a crib legit wit' no pressure," Lyric remarked, offering inspiration. Lyric being a diabolical genius in the industry understood the diversity of college students residing in Tallahassee, which would possibly broaden his fan base countrywide.

"Alright dats a bet. I'mma ride out in a few days, but I'll let you know when I touch down in da city," Youngin' said, slapping five and coming toward an embrace with both brothers. After ending the brief conversation, Youngin' loaded the boxes into the Range Rover and took off through the streets, destined for his father's garage. On arrival, he was greeted by his three remaining and focused loyal teammates posted up in the parking lot. Solo was about five foot ten, dark skin, pudgy build and bald-headed with twelve gold teeth complemented by a thick beard. He sorta resembled a down south Freeway. Will was more of a pretty thug, but he was very dangerous if underestimated. He stood an even six foot two with a light skin complexion, along with thick, neat dreadlocks that are known in South Florida as bombays. Speed, who received his name during his many years of playing running back in Pop Warner football, stood an even six feet tall, an almond complexion coated his skin, with a cornrow braided hairstyle and eight gold teeth done by the legendary Dr. Kelly; two on his top canines and six at the bottom.

"What's poppin, Five?" Youngin' asked.

"Five alive, but as you know J.B. ain't. Da alligators on I-75 probably done chewed him bones and all by now," Solo replied.

"Dats real, so who truck dis is?" Youngin' asked, referring to the grey Cadillac Escalade they were riding in.

"Oh dis shit is a rental, but dem bitches made me pay an extra fee for being under twenty-five," Solo responded. "So what da lick read?"

"We gon' slide up to Orlando and wait there fa you to lead da way, but before we blaze, we need ya new phone number so we know to move."

"Y'all moving and thinking like some real niggas and I respect dat. Dis the number," Youngin' said as Solo locked the number in.

Youngin' continued stating, "By the way, take a box of dese mixtapes wit' you. If you pass thru da mall or da flea market, pass 'em around fa me. Shit jamming, ya smell me. As a matter of fact, pop one in," Youngin' said grinning.

"Fasho big homie, you know we gon' represent." Will spoke, giving dap simultaneously.

"Straight up. Ay y'all boys burn da road, but soon as y'all buy dem new phones, bark at me ASAP so I know everything hood," Youngin' stated.

"Fasho," Solo responded. As his little homies rode off, Youngin's old cellphone vibrated in his pocket and when he glanced at the caller screen he became very hostile.

"Talk!" Youngin' exclaimed.

"Five in da morning. Same spot," Mr. Brown remarked.

"Just be there chump!"

"Same to you pussy mutha..." Mr. Brown was stating before Youngin' slammed the phone down on the concrete, shattering it to pieces. Youngin' then pulled out his other phone and dialed a different number.

"Change of the time. It's going down at 5:00 a.m. so let Unc know wassup."

"Alright," Pops replied while laying back in the bed at the Hard Rock Resort, getting fellatio action from Charlene. Once he hung up the phone, Youngin' instantly jumped back in the car to dial a different caller.

"What's up, you home?" He waited for a response then spoke again. "Aight, I'm 'bout to fall through in twenty minutes." Youngin' fired up the remainder of the blunt he had in the ashtray and coasted through the nightlife.

Chapter 21

"Damn girl, you know you a sexy muthafucka right?" Youngin' stated as he walked through the front door. He was blown away by how the light purple laced boy shorts underwear set dropped across Shaun's body.

"But see, dats where a bitch like me keep weak niggas fooled because I'm real like a killer," she stated, spinning around exposing the small .22 concealed on the back of her thick thigh tucked in a light purple gun holster. Youngin' was mesmerized by the way her ass cheeks seemed to swallow the crease of the underwear with each step taken, not to mention her 42-inch ass.

"I don't want no trouble," Youngin' replied playfully, throwing both palms up in the air.

"Bae you know I'm down fa you, but I must stay on point being that I live alone. You know dese crazy ass dudes been preying on single females, especially the fine ones too," Shaun responded, laying the pistol on the counter doing a model-like 360 degree spin. Shaun lived in a moderate, gated apartment community located on Ives Dairy Road, and it was very much cozy. When Youngin' called to tell her that he was coming through, she altered her normal routine of being naked, switching to a more seducing outfit.

"You definitely fine, boo. By da way, did you get dat for me?" Youngin' asked.

"Yeah, I'm 'bout to show up," Shaun replied turning to go in the bedroom as the purple velvet material pumps clocked against the tile kitchen floor. Youngin' was rolling a blunt when Shaun re-entered the living room carrying a black Nike duffel bag. She dropped it on the floor directly in front of him. Youngin' was momentarily dazed, licking the blunt and holding it front of him. His attention was captured by Shaun's pussy lips that seemed to be sucking the satin boy shorts inside.

"Put ya tongue in your mouth and check it out," Shaun stated, giggling and reaching for the television remote control. Youngin' looked up at her shaking his head, impressed that this woman had an effect on him that few women were capable of attaining. Shaun was scanning through the channels but came to a halt on Channel 7 News station.

"Damn boo, you see dis shit! Dem Zoes got jammed up at da Port of Miami with over 400 bricks and got away," Shaun stated, gaining Youngin's attention.

Once he realized the Haitian that got caught up was his connect, he shouted, "Oh shit, dem niggas! Damn, dese crackas done killed my dawgs."

"It's crazy out here in these streets right now so I know it's time to get away for a while."

"Yeah you right, bae," Youngin' remarked, staring down at the bundles of counterfeit money. Before Shaun could change the channel, another exclusive story grasped her attention.

"I'm reporting live outside the MDPD building with a breaking news pertaining to a long time narcotics agent who is facing a federal indictment for aiding and abetting drug dealers while also being involved in a prostitution ring. Earlier, authorities received an anonymous video for the ex-officer you see on the photo named Mr. Brown, exchanging innumerable sums of cash for sexual favors. We are not allowed to broadcast the video, but it's rumored that one of the women on the tape is the deceased white female, Cristin Summers, who was found murdered just days ago. Authorities believe this may be a related incident, but have yet to release further information..." were the words spoken by the reporter on the scene before Youngin' spoke again.

"Damn, karma is a bitch. Dats da same slimy sucka that's been leeching off me all dis time. But I got him tho because his ass won't be laughing when he get a hold of dis funny money," he said grinning devilishly, preparing for not just his vengeance but his father's long awaited redemption as well.

"Fuck all dat bullshit. I want some dick," Shaun stated grabbing at Youngin'.

"You can get dat boo," Youngin' replied, passing her the blunt. He then bent down between her legs and placed each one on his shoulders while gripping her thighs from behind. He pulled her satin panties to the side and began to lick and suck her juices as if he was a thirsty camel in the desert, only he took his time flicking her gentle clit back in forth as well in circular motions with his moist tongue. Shaun wasn't sure if the weed or the sexual sensation gave her the high she felt, but whatever it was she never wanted it to stop.

"Bae, I'm about to..." Shaun stated, but was cut off when Youngin' stood up and fired up the unlit blunt she was holding.

"Why you stopped?" Shaun cooed. Youngin' stood smiling as Shaun was literally begging for some more of the sexual morphine doses, seeking an orgasm. Youngin' did this exact ritual for forty-five minutes straight, and every time Shaun was on the verge of having an orgasm he would stop, making her scream out for more. This pussy-licking tactic was a build-up, so upon taking her over the edge Shaun moaned for at least five seconds, "Aaaah-unnh-aaah," while skeeting like a pressure cleaner for the first time in her young sexual experience. Standing to drop articles of clothing,

Youngin' sat down on the couch with his dick standing straight up, saluting her. She didn't hesitate to suck his dick like it was the last Tootsie Roll Pop in stock.

While Shaun was sucking Youngin' into a frenzy, he used his right index and pointer finger to play inside her pussy, causing her to suck his dick passionately due to the mind-blowing experience. Before Shaun knew it, Youngin' stood up and raised her pussy to his face while she was upside down facing his penis, performing the sixty-nine position while standing. They both came simultaneously as Youngin' slid back down the couch slowly. After Shaun wiped his dick clean with her mouth, she slid down his sweaty chest like a slip-n-slide, placing her wet, neatly shaved pussy atop his dick with her palms on the carpet and began to ride him like a stick shift convertible. Before fucking in doggy-style position, Youngin' used his fingers to keep her pussy wet while Shaun wobbled her ass to give him a round of applause for his sexual performance. Youngin' placed his moist fingers in her mouth as she licked every crevice while he slid his dick into her tight, warm pussy.

"Oooh shit… yes, put dat dick in me daddy. Yes, Yes, Yes fuck me!" Shaun screamed in ecstasy.

Around 1:30 a.m., after two hours of energizing sex, Youngin' stated, "Bae you gon cook ya boy some breakfast?"

"Yes, but lemme go clean myself up first. You know I don't eat pork? I got turkey bacon tho."

"Dats straight," Youngin' replied.

"Aight, give me a minute."

Fifteen minutes later, Shaun exited the shower with her hair in a ponytail, wearing black undergarments. She kept her word and cooked a light breakfast that consisted of turkey bacon, eggs, grits, and toast.

"Let's go ahead and get dressed so we can get outta here," Youngin' remarked once they finished eating. Shaun came out dressed in some tight black denim jeans, a pair of all-black Nike Air Max and a tight Gucci navel-length leather jacket. She loaded about ten suitcases into the Rover containing clothes, shoes, jewelry and pictures of her deceased family members that she valued mostly.

"I'mma follow behind you 'cause I wanna load my bike up on da U-Haul," Shaun stated, referring to her personalized red and black Yamaha motorcycle. "Fasho, but what you do wit ya auto?" Youngin' asked.

"Oh, I let my lil' cousin keep it because she graduate in about a month from South Broward High School, so it was a graduation present."

"Dats real cause dat Acura fly as fuck. Anyways, let's ride out and stay on schedule," Youngin' replied walking out to the car destined for the location where the U-Haul with a car trailer attached was parked. Once they arrived, Youngin' loaded all of Shaun's belongings onto the U-Haul then strapped the Range Rover down on the back exactly how it was shown in the manual. Excellent with preparation, Pops had a separate vehicle waiting at the exact same location, so Youngin' and Shaun split up as she took the U-Haul to the Holiday Inn off Broward Boulevard as instructed by Youngin', getting a room while waiting on his return.

Youngin' arrived at the designated meeting place in North Miami Beach as his dad and uncle were already awaiting. As the all-black 2008 Dodge Caravan arrived, Pops and Riley loaded up, never speaking a word, only silently dapping one another. Youngin' knew for a fact that his dad and uncle were experienced at missions as such due to the calming aura they exuberated. They waited for their target in the parking lot for about forty-five minutes, surveying the area and continuing the temporary silence. Upon deep contemplation, Youngin' decided not to say a word within Mr. Brown's car because he was possibly wired.

Once Youngin' saw the Cadillac CTS headlights pulling in, he waited for Mr. Brown to park then pulled in a couple spaces down from him. Youngin' got in the car, tossed him the black gym bag and looked into his bloodshot eyes, then got out, never speaking a word. The redness of Mr. Brown's eyes was a result of being up all night snorting coke and drinking whiskey in an attempt to drown out the misery he felt from the recent problems.

The ex-officer of the law had his head down counting the bundles of money and suddenly raised it hastily, shouting, "What the fuck!" Before Mr. Brown could reach under the driver seat for his pistol to step down on Youngin', the driver side window was shattered by the butt end of a Mossberg pump. He was never allowed to counter-react because the round barrel was leveled off with the center of his forehead, as a second masked assassin stood positioned on the passenger side of the car aiming an AK-47 rifle at him.

"Get out the fuckin' car now!" Mr. Brown carefully obliged, fearful of making any hasty movements, hoping they wouldn't kill him. Riley, holding the AK-47, came around the back of the car and stood in front of Mr. Brown as Pops standing behind suddenly struck Mr. Brown's cranium, knocking him unconscious with the butt end of the pump. Then, he used Mr. Brown's spare cuffs to shackle him. Pops grabbed the only linking evidence, which his son left behind with possible DNA on it; the black duffel bag draping across his right shoulder. Youngin' drove up with the caravan's side door wide open as Pops and Riley hoisted Mr. Brown's huge body into the caravan, then casually drove away from the scene of the crime as the Cadillac STS's ignition continued to remain on with the car's gear shift in park.

Inside the auto with gloved hands, Riley duct taped his mouth and wrapped his legs together as if he were a deer being prepared for roots over a camp fire. They arrived at a secluded warehouse parking lot that was abandoned near the Skylake plaza dollar movie cinema; it was at least fifteen minutes away from the original body snatching grounds. Upon coming to a halt, the trio of family members exited the caravan to the rear and prepared to walk Mr. Brown back to life.

"Wake up bitch!" shouted Youngin', using his leather Nike baseball gloved palm to slap the left side open, fearful for his life. Trying to chew through the duct tape, Mr. Brown mumbled in a frenzy, "Mmm, mmm, mmm," nearly having a shortage of breath.

"Listen, I'mma pull this off but if you so much as talk too loud he gonna put a bullet through ya dome, understand?" Youngin' stated, reaching to peel off the duct tape as Mr. Brown nodded in agreement. Riley stood to Youngin's right side with the AK-47 aimed at his third eye.

"Huuuh," Mr. Brown quietly exhaled then inhaled thankful for the breath of air seeping through his dry-cracked, parched lips. Pops stood with the Mossberg pump parallel with his right side, simultaneously raising the black cotton ski mask to his hairline, staring at his most hated enemy.

"Do you know who dis is?" Youngin' asked Mr. Brown, pointing with his right index finger to his left side counterpart. Mr. Brown was shaking his head in a horizontal motion.

"No, I don't know him and I don't know what this is all about. Please don't kill me."

"Sure you remember your very first alleged Kingpin, don't you? You testified against sending him to prison," Pops stated, handing Youngin' the pump. Upon recognition, Mr. Brown spoke again with fear chilling his blood.

"I, I was only doing my job." He was shuttering in the process of attempting to offer an excuse.

"Seems to me you got a hard-on when da judge gave me dat time cause you and da State Attorney were high fivin' while I was in turmoil leaving a wife and son behind," Pops stated, causing Mr. Brown to momentarily tense up before being yanked from the rear of the cab. Pops slammed the back of his skull on the concrete. Mr. Brown was in pain, but more upset with himself for not recognizing the resemblance of Youngin' to Pops.

"And to think yo' punk ass been trying to put down on my son. Dats where you fucked up! Bitch nigga don't you know my wife died while I was in prison, plus I couldn't get no pussy for twelve years. But dats all good 'cause now I'm fuckin your wife Charlene, you pussy muthafucka!" Pops stated venomously, sending chills down the spine of those whose ears caught wind of the remark.

"I'mma kill you!" Mr. Brown yelled before losing his voice momentarily as Pops used his steel-toe boots to kick him in the nuts, as if David Beckham himself was attempting to score a penalty kick in the Soccer World Cup. Mr. Brown's beefy wrists were still cuffed behind his back so he couldn't even soothe his aching scrotum sack. Instead of giving him a chance to alleviate the pain, Pops kneeled down to wrap his huge hands around Mr. Brown's neck, using his knuckles to beat him in the face until he was unconscious.

"Finish that off," Pops stated, arising with blood dripping from the black gloves. Riley shoved the barrel of the AK-47 down Mr. Brown's mouth, pulling the trigger once as four piercing shells spewed out into his cranium. The trio rode away from the murder scene, leaving the deceased human carnage on the asphalt to possibly feed the fowls of the air and the starring scavengers roaming the Earth.

No one spoke a word for at least five minutes, until Youngin' lightened the mood stating, "Damn Pops, you smashin' da nigga wife?" smiling simultaneously.

Smiling, Pops responded, "Yeah I found out last night after fucking her over a week. We was watchin' da headlines last night and when she saw him on TV, she laced me up on the situation. She ain't know I was 'bout to do him in and she'll never know. But yeah ol' girl fine as hell tho."

"If you talking about the lady from the casino, she definitely is badd," Riley remarked from the backseat.

"Be easy big bruh, you already got a gorgeous sista on ya arms," Pops responded, jokingly showing no evident signs of being a dangerous man. Quickly the mood inside the van shifted as they began to discuss women, a subject in which they all were fond of. Riley was nearly having an out of body experience as he was in deep thought about his wife and daughters, but mainly having a premonition pertaining to his plan to seduce his wife when he made it home. While they were driving, Youngin' called a yellow cab and told them he needed a ride from Footmart U.S.A. in

Hollywood in order to trek to the hotel off Broward Boulevard, where Shaun awaited his safe arrival.

Chapter 22

"Here you go," Youngin' stated, handing Shaun a caramel flavored coffee from Starbucks as he was getting into the front seat of the U-Haul. Youngin' gulped down the ice cold Red Bull energy drink, then rolled down the window with the air conditioner on high while he lit a wine-flavored Black & Mild cigar. They were parked at Turkey Lake rest stop along Florida's Turnpike just outside Orlando while they waited for Will, Solo and Speed to arrive so they could take off.

"Lemme hit dat black boo," Shaun said, placing a bookmark on the page she was reading before sitting the novel atop the dashboard. Youngin' passed it to her, holding onto it loosely with his index and middle finger combined.

"What you reading? It looked like some hood shit," he said glancing at the book cover.

"It is and it's good too. It's called *Loyal 2 Da Money* by Imonie Sincere," Shaun replied as her body language exuberated the words 'You gotta read it!'
"Imonie Sincere, huh? I'mma check it out and see if we eye-to-eye on our literature game boo," Youngin' remarked, grinning as his cellphone rang bringing his consciousness back to the present. He regained his military mind state, aware that with

one mistake his team would be suffering a major setback.

"Where y'all at?" Youngin' asked.

"We pulling in right now," Solo responded.

"Aight, I see y'all," Youngin' replied, noticing the Cadillac SUV veering off the turnpike.

"Ay, but don't park 'cause we outta here. Follow me and be the eyes behind my head," Youngin' concluded, hanging up to navigate the oversized U-Haul vehicle.

While they trekked upstate towards the panhandle, Shaun relaxed quietly reading the novel in spurts while multi-tasking being an extra set of eyes for Youngin'. Eventually needing to gas up, they made a brief stop at Shell gas station in Gainesville just off the Archer Road exit and noticed the abrupt change of atmosphere amongst the people.

"Damn bae, you seen dat country ass nigga wit da finger waves and dat fake ass chain tryin' to holla?" Shaun said, laughing uncontrollably and passing Youngin' the Sprite soda as they merged back onto I-75 northbound.

After taking a swig of the soda, Youngin' stated, "Just be alert 'cause dudes similar to his pedigree be working for da people."

"Yeah you right," Shaun replied, understanding the severity of just one simple mistake. The radio clock within the U-Haul read 6:58 p.m. as they were exiting Interstate-10 in the Leon County city limits. Youngin' was conversing on his cell with Lyric, receiving directions to Hampton Inn while traveling south on N.E. Capital Circle Road. Once they arrived, Shaun entered the hotel and purchased the family size suite on the fifth floor.

On one side of the suite was a huge bedroom with three twin beds and a huge bathroom. The other side held a queen-size bed with an oversized bathroom complemented by a stand-up shower. A kitchen and a dining room was also included, releasing the home sweet home ambiance.

After resting inside the dining area for about ten minutes discussing how long the drive was, Will spoke up. "I don't know about y'all, but I'm hungry den a muthafucka!"

"You ain't lying 'bout dat. So what y'all wanna eat?" Youngin' asked.

"I seen a T.G.I.Friday's when we was on da way in. They sell alcohol and I could definitely use one," Shaun replied, offering a suggestion to the group.

"Yeah dats straight. Let's hit it 'cause I'm starving my damn self," Solo remarked. The entourage of five loaded up in the Cadillac Escalade leaving the U-Haul parked at the far end of the hotel parking lot.

"Ay, put on da radio station so we can get a feel for the atmosphere up dis way," Youngin' stated from the backseat, understanding that one could tell a lot about a certain environment by the music alone. "I think Lyric said it's 102.3 FM if I ain't mistaken." From the passenger seat Speed did the tuning, halting on the exact station mentioned as the radio host was speaking.

"What's happenin' Tallahassee? It's ya favorite DJ 1-Champ coming back to you live with da top eight at eight countdown. Remember to write down all the songs you hear and be our tenth caller for a chance to win two free tickets to Danny Boi's album release party..." Upon his labelmate's name being mentioned, Youngin' maintained a very attentive ear.

"Before we get onto the number five song on da countdown, we got a bonus track for da streets. Ay, guest DJ for the night representin' Tallahassee, introduce the song fa da streets," DJ 1-Champ stated, pausing to allow the lucky caller for the night to help host.

"Hey Tallahassee, it's ya girl Ki-Ki and I want y'all to turn up ya radio and rip da knobs off as one of our own, Danny Boi, blazes the radio on Blazin 102.3!"

Upon hearing the beat, Youngin' maintained a humble confidence. "Ay yo turn it up! That shit sound like it's gon' be fire," he said, already knowing that it was the track he recorded with Danny Boi. Everybody in the car was bobbing their heads unaware that in thirty seconds Youngin's verse would put more fuel to flame.

They were at a stop light when Speed intuitively blurted out, "Damn big homie, dat sounds like you!"

Youngin' just grinned as all eyes in the truck were focused on him, seeking confirmation. While laughing, he said, "Aight, aight it was me, but if y'all niggas would have listened to da mixtape I gave you, you would have heard the song. That's my labelmate song, but I added it as a bonus track on da mixtape."

"Man we was vibin' to 2Pac and Soulja Slim on da way up. We ain't know it was for real like dat," Solo replied as he mashed the gas pedal when the stop light switched to green.

"Well now y'all niggas know ain't no games being played. We gon' do what we do best, but dis rap shit is first priority. No mistakes allowed!" Youngin' stated with an advisory expression upon his countenance, assuring everyone that handling business was important.

"There go the restaurant right there. Let's go get dis grub," Will said, pointing to the left in the direction of the semi-crowded restaurant bar.

"Y'all eat as much as you want. Everything on me," Youngin' stated, as the entourage exited the vehicle rubbing their bellies. No one objected to Youngin's offer as they walked through the glass doors of the restaurant, maintaining a certain aura that only the wealthy in society seemed to obtain. One thing that separated them from contenders was the humble, confident, hood rich swag.

Chapter 23

"Damn big homie, shit jamming!" Speed stated while sitting in the passenger seat of the rental truck, bobbing his head and keeping the Backwood stuffed with dro in rotation within the vehicle. Will, the lightest reflection in the hazy smoked filled car, stated, "Yeah I'm definitely vibin' bruh-bruh."

"Damn fool, it's a lot of badd ass bitches goin' in dat shit," Solo exclaimed pointing towards one of the many entrances of the Governor's Square Mall.

"We gon' slide in there in a minute. Just be easy," Will replied from the backseat, laughing at his homeboy's beast-like nature.

"Ain't no pressure," Solo responded, regaining his composure and realizing that down at the bottom of the map seeing flocks of top-notch women is common. In the midst of their inconspicuous eye-candy viewing and smoke session, Solo's phone vibrated on his lap.

"What they do?" Solo asked, placing the phone atop the center console on speaker.

"Vibin', taking care of business, but where y'all boys at?"

"Bout to fall off in da mall, wassup?"

"Type in Best Buy on Apalachee Parkway on your GPS, then y'all slide through ASAP."

"I think we on Apalachee Parkway now." Speed spoke up in the background, remembering the street sign he saw earlier.   "Damn, y'all niggas got me on speaker?" Youngin' asked, laughing lightly. Before anyone could respond he continued, "Ay, but y'all slide through so we can take care of this."

"Yeah."

After typing in the address, they followed the route that was relayed via the GPS device. Will suddenly noticed the huge yellow and blue Best Buy sign before their eyes.

"Damn, there go dat shit right there!"

As they reared slowly into the huge parking lot, they spotted Youngin' posted up on the hood of a burgundy two-door Pontiac G6 talking on his cellphone. The trio parked a few spaces down before approaching Youngin', just as he was ending his phone conversation.

"What's hood wit y'all boys?"

"Just scoping out da scenery like real niggas do", Will replied.

"I done made a few power moves, mostly important getting y'all a spot to live down da street from where I'm staying at."

"Dat was a real power move being dat we just touched down yesterday," Speed replied.

"We bussin' out here, connected everywhere we plant our feet ya smell me. By da way, here go y'all keys to da spot," Youngin' stated, reaching through the ajar window as Shaun, who was sitting with her feet perched on the dashboard, handed over three sets of keys. "Y'all take these and follow me 'cause a couple delivery trucks gon' be bringing furniture. I just paid the Geek Squad to stop thru and set up all the T.V. and computer equipment so I need y'all to be there," Youngin' stated.

"Aight, we out," Solo stated, as everyone turned in unison headed back to the SUV. Fifteen minutes later, Youngin' pulled to the side of the road in a semi-suburban area named Southwood. Youngin' stepped out the car and approached the driver side window of the truck.

"Dats y'all crib ova there, 1205," he directed, pointing with an index finger to one of the many three-car garage townhomes in the area. "I gotta roll out, but once everythang is done, y'all do what you do. I'll link up wit y'all later." Youngin' turned to leave but halted to continue speaking. "Oh yeah, y'all be easy out here 'cause we don't need much heat."

"Don't worry we gon' be under da radar moving like real niggas move in silence, ya smell me," Solo responded, never cracking the slightest grin.

"Alright y'all hold it down," Youngin' concluded, dapping everyone through the window.

Finally inside, everyone strolled around surveying the pad. "Damn dis shit tight!" Speed exclaimed, excitedly impressed by the Block Boyz domain. The entire spot was laid out with plush, beige carpet, except for the kitchen and dining area, which was a cookies and cream colored marble tile. There was also a loft area that resembled a third floor, allowing one to look down below the previous two levels.

"Yeah dis bitch definitely on point," Solo remarked.

Hearing the doorbell sound off, Will shouted out, "I got it. There's a truck outside with Ashley Furniture logos so dats probably fa us." He trotted downstairs.

Once Will signed the delivery forms, he permitted the movers to haul in the bedroom sets, the suede black furniture along with the glass coffee tables. Before they were finished bringing in the furniture, a billiard company was parked outside with their property, along with a white Geek Squad van representing Best Buy's superior services. An hour later, the interior of the townhouse was arrayed with everything possible to allow each of the young men to be comfortable.

"What's up, y'all niggas hungry?" Will asked.

"Hell yeah, let's go to dat Publix I seen when we was sliding in," Solo replied.

"How 'bout we just find a Wal-Mart so I can get some sheets for my bed at da same time," Speed remarked.

"Sounds like a plan to me. Type it in ya phone GPS system and let's roll," Solo replied as everyone walked out to the car.

Chapter 24

"Yeah big bruh, it was so many broads in there last night," Speed stated, getting somewhat excited.

"In Wal-Mart?" Youngin' asked, curiously.

"Yeah bruh, I think they about to start a new semester at da college campuses 'cause it wasn't nothing but students in there shopping."

"Y'all niggas ain't holla at none of dem?" Youngin' asked, causing Will and Solo to cease their pool game nearby.

Will intruded the conversational cypher. "Be fa real bruh, now you know how we do. We some intellectual real niggas and we understand dat da females are our way in."

"Aight, I'm glad y'all were thinkin' with the proper mindstate."

"Yeah, round 'bout 12:30 we going out to FAMU to pass out some CDs on some promotional shit. They got some shit going on. Um, what they call dat shit, Lo?" Will asked.

"Every Friday all da students be hanging out on da set, dat broad I hollered at said," Solo responded.

"Dats real. But shit, y'all turn dat rental in on Tuesday 'cause y'all whips gon' be out da shop. I'm 'bout to bounce, but I'll bark at y'all boys later. I gotta go handle some business," Youngin' stated, dapping his partners before leaving.

At approximately 12:45 p.m., Will, Solo and Speed were exiting the Cadillac Escalade that they parked in the lot surrounding Bragg stadium on Florida A&M University's campus.

"Excuse me beautiful, but can you tell me how to get to the set?" Will asked the Nubian sister getting out the Volkswagen Jetta with the Michigan license plate right next to them.

"Yeah, it's all the way at the top of the hill across campus. You'll see all the people out there," she replied, pointing in the direction.

"Thank you, but uh… you not going?"

"I'mma pass thru there, but I gotta go to this journalism course."

"Dats real, but if I may ask, what's your major?"

"Architecture, 'cause my passion is to design home blueprints and my minor is Journalism."

"Dats wassup. Well, since you're a busy woman, I refuse to waste your precious time, but if you feel as if you have the stamina to pick up an extra study, I'd love to call you."

"Yeah, that's cool. My number is (313) 206-9597 and my name is Makayla. And you?"

"My name is Will and that's my number flashing across your screen now," he replied, pointing towards the Verizon Droid secured on her hip.

"Alright, I got it and I'll call you when you get out of class," Makayla replied, shaking Will's extended right hand before walking off.

"Damn lil mama bad," Solo stated as they were walking in the direction of the set.

"Yeah, she got dat exotic, up-north look ya dig," Will responded. The trio was wearing white, low-top shell toe Adidas, army fatigue cargo shorts and white T-shirts with an army green design. The 'Dynamic Duo' logo was pressed on the front. Each one of them also had a Gucci book bag with one-hundred CDs that they planned to give away free of cost. They were posted up near the Orange Room, which is actually an on-campus Rattler branded restaurant that served quality food.

"Damn, it's hot out here," Solo stated, wiping his bald head with the white towel he had draped over his right shoulder.

"Dese broads been sweating some real niggas too," Speed arrogantly stated, walking up to a dude passing out a CD.

"Yeah, I see. Plus, you realize how all over town different lil college parties poppin'," Solo responded.

"They think we students too, which is good 'cause dats how we gon' fool da streets to keep our Block Boyz shit bumpin', ya smell me," Will stated.

"Yeah I feel dat, but right now I'm 'bout to snatch lil' mama right dere," Solo said, approaching a young lady coming from the Tucker Hall building on the campus where classes were held.

At approximately 3:00 p.m., they were leaving the campus blazing up some of that fire marijuana that could only be found in the Dade and Broward County area codes, while discussing all the phone numbers they managed to possess. Instead of typing a specific location, Will just drove around town scoping how things around the Capital City operated, mainly the hood traffic. Eventually, they needed to hit up a Waffle House located on Tennessee Street because Solo's hunger pain became unbearable. They rested there until they decided to type in their home address, allowing the GPS device to guide them back.

The time was nearing 6:30 as the trio began making calculated phone calls, also debating whether or not they'd be in attendance at THE EDGE, the nightclub DJ EZONE was heavily promoting while dee-jaying on the set.

"Shaun, wassup witcha?" Solo asked as they were stepping through the front door.

"Vibin' like a badd bitch do. Dat boy Youngin' in da kitchen cooking. Speed, lock da door behind you," Shaun replied, walking towards the kitchen.

"What they do soldiers?" Youngin' asked, as he was pulling garlic biscuits out the oven.

"Whateva we tell 'em. But shit, wassup wit da grub?" Will responded, rubbing his belly from the mouth-watering aroma permeating his nasal passages.

"Everything will be done in 'bout five minutes. After we get done eating, I'mma holla at y'all 'bout what I called y'all over here for."

"Fasho," Will replied. Youngin' never bragged much about his cooking but while his dad was away in prison, his mother had taught him certain recipes that would make women hold their panties in the air and dudes would tip their hats to him after the meal. This particular night, he prepared an exclusive pot of jambalaya that was flavored with chopped turkey sausage, shrimp, diced peppers, red peppers, cilantro leaves, brown rice, various spicy Creole seasonings and a few extra added ingredients he chose not to reveal.

"Damn big bruh, you need to teach me how to burn like dis 'cause bitches get wet instantly off some shit like dis," Speed stated with a mouthful of food. Shaun began to blush because his words were truthful. Once they finished eating, everyone sat in the living room passing blunts around while sipping Patron with Red Bull Energy Drink chaser as Youngin' had his label mate Danny Boi's album playing.

"Aight, dis what da lick read. I'mma put da dope in ya life like I been doin', ya smell me. I talked to my dawg today and he certified y'all to set up shop in his hood where it's been a drought the last few years 'cause he had to leave town on some other matters. Tomorrow, y'all gone scope the area to learn da surroundings. It's y'all job to show dese country cool ass niggas how to trap. Don't get me wrong, it's some real niggas up here and dem da ones who gonna come shop. Five in da morning til five in da evening and after dat, shop closed! Don't even open da trap on Tuesdays and Thursdays," Youngin' explained.

"We gon' need more den dese glocks to hold da block down just in case dese dudes disrespect da set and fuck up da money, smell me," Speed remarked.

"I got all dat taken care of lil' homie, so don't trip. Niggas up here ain't territorial like dat, but we always gonna be on point."

"Ain't no pressure, big homie, we da Block Boyz so you know dis what we do best," Solo stated.

"I already know dat. In 'bout two months y'all gon' meet Danny Boi when he come up top for his album release party. Until then, we gonna get the flyers and promotions circulating, ya dig. We gon' be real busy, but it is what it is."

"Shit, you got dem flyers on deck already?" Will asked.

"Yeah, wassup?"

"Let's hit da let out fa THE EDGE and pass 'em out 'cause a nigga kinda wanna get at some of dese intellectual college shones." "Aight, I'm wit dat, but we gonna slide in da Rover 'cause I got posters of bruh album cover on da back windows," Youngin' replied.

"Dats a bet! I'mma GPS it on my phone," Will remarked.

"Shit, I'm wit dat too. I think dude was sayin' it's South Monroe Street, wherever dats at," Solo stated.

The four of them loaded up with Youngin' and drove to the Southside of Tallahassee, destined for the night club scene.

Chapter 25

Approximately two months since their initial touchdown, Youngin' and the Block Boyz had the streets set ablaze with the product they were moving. On this particular day, the Block Boyz chose to fall back in order to enjoy the ground-breaking success of Dynamic Duo Entertainment's lead artist, Danny Boi. Will, Solo, and Speed were at their pad entertaining three lovely ladies from Atlanta that were students at Florida State University. The surround sound system was mellowed out as it was tuned into the local radio station, Blazin 102.3. Moments before the top eight at eight countdown, Danny Boi was in the building conducting a live interview.

"What's happenin', 850? It's ya boy 1-Champ holdin' it down, doin' what I do. I want you to call ya homegirl, call ya momma, call ya sista, call whoever and let them know we got Tallahassee's own Danny Boi in da building. Danny Boi, what's going on, how you feeling?"

"First of all, let me say I'm feelin' great. My debut album hit stores today, so if you ain't got it, go get dat! Big ups to da whole 850 showin' love. Y'all come out and party wit' me tonight at da Moon. Big ups to the entire Dynamic Duo family, da Block Boyz, da lovely ladies, Supastar J-Kwik, of course 1-Champ and da whole Blazin family for showin' me love and to anybody and everybody that got love for Danny Boi."

"Dats real. Well listen, we can't keep da people waiting so why don't you go ahead and introduce a hit single fa us," 1-Champ stated, enthusiastically.

"What it is, Capital City, my city, yo city da only city dat keep it Blazin. This my new single from my brand new album titled *Judgin' Me*. Turn ya radios up and rip da knobs off 'cause it's Dynamic!" Danny stated over the airwaves as the DJ spun the record upon his last word.

At the townhouse, Speed was using the radio remote control to crank the system up a few notches after hearing Danny Boi shout out the family. After the song was over, Solo's phone rang.

"What they do? ... Uh huh ... Alright, we on da way." Solo walked away from the pool table. "Ay Will, Speed, bruh want us to come holla at dem."

"Aight, lemme go change clothes real quick and I'll be ready," Will replied.

"Yeah, I'mma do da same," Speed stated.

"Fasho. Ay ladies, before y'all leave take these V.I.P tickets to come vibe at da Moon tonight wit' Danny Boi," Solo advised, passing the ladies three tickets.

"Oooh, we 'bout to go get ready too then," the tall redbone stated with excitement. Forty five minutes later, Will, Solo and Speed arrived downtown in front of the DoubleTree Hotel in assembly line fashion, all driving black-on-black Cadillac CTS model cars with 23-inch black alloy rims, complemented by Lamborghini doors. They valet parked directly in front of the hotel and trekked upstairs via elevator to the eighteenth floor where everyone was located in a huge, elegant suite. Lyric, Danny Boi, Shay, Jamilah, Youngin' and Shaun were inside the room. They had three ice buckets with bottles of Rosé on chill as they were vibing and preparing to make sure everyone knew Dynamic Duo is a label to be reckoned with.

"There they go! Da Block Boyz in da building," Danny Boi shouted, making them feel like celebs themselves. Danny Boi had met the Block Boyz about a month ago when he made his return to town to purchase a home in Killearn Estates.

The moment Danny Boi was in their presence, he felt the vibe that only real niggas could comprehend. For the last month, he'd been watching via an unknown source and was appreciative of the way they'd been handling operations pertaining to Dynamic Duo Entertainment, as well as their hustle tactics in the unfamiliar streets.

"What they do, big homie?" Solo stated, dapping Danny Boi up as he continued around the room greeting everyone else. Will and Speed followed suit.

"Man we up in dis bitch vibin' before we head ova there," Danny responded, pausing for a second. "Ay before y'all get ya drank on, I wanna ask y'all some questions while everybody here," he continued.

"We all ears," Will replied.

"You know I fucks wit y'all young niggas, ya dig. Y'all got ya own swag, you niggas runnin' like bosses in ya lane. And y'all 'bout money. My only question is are y'all willing to be loyal to dis Dynamic Duo movement?"

"Wit us, it's death before dishonor, always," Speed assured him for the group, as they nodded their head in agreement.

"I feel dat, so I wanna bring y'all into da family proper. Jamilah, bring me dat black box," Danny Boi requested. On cue, Jamilah approached with a shoe-sized black box that had three red diamond, platinum Dynamic Duo medallion chains. When Danny Boi draped the links around their necks one by one, it hung just below the torso portion of their chests.

"Like a referee, it's official. By da way, I know y'all don't rap, but eventually I want y'all to come by da studio and work with Lyric 'cause I believe it's talent stored inside y'all. But listen, y'all know it's my night so let's go represent fa da Double D fam."

"Man I just wanna thank you and da big homie Youngin' fa everythang, straight up," Will stated, admiring everyone's iced out label pieces.

"Dats nothing. Y'all just stay on ya grind and life will be great," Danny Boi replied.

"To Danny Boi!" Youngin' shouted, holding up a bottle of Rosé, as everyone else feeling swaggerific did the same.

The all black six-car convoy was riding down Apalachee Parkway making a right turn on Magnolia Drive, then another quick right on St. Augustine Road in order to allow a grand entrance arrival at the club. The three Cadillac CTS automobiles led the way, followed by Lyric and Danny Boi in a two-door coupe Porsche Carrera 911. Shay and Jamilah were behind them in a matching coupe while Youngin' and Shaun reared the park in the Range Rover. The exterior of the club was crowded with people ready to go in. Instead of creeping through the side entrance, they parked directly in front of the club and walked through the V.I.P crowd, as if Moses himself followed by the Israelites were passing through a parted Red Sea. Danny Boi was in his element as he chucked deuces and shook hands on his way in.

As the entourage strolled through, everyone in attendance was taking pictures with their camera phones, simply amazed by the down–to-earth personalities of the Dynamic Duo Family. Upon entering the dimly lit club, the entourage went directly to their designated VIP area, immediately popping bottles while posing in fly mode to the electrifying vibe, as usual. At about one o'clock, Lyric led the way from the upper deck section of the Moon down to the stage below. Lyric informed the staff that for the next hour everybody would receive free Hennessy, compliments of the host.

When Danny Boi grabbed the mic and began talking, the women went berserk and attempted to reach for his genitals from below the stage. Danny Boi performed six songs from his album, including the track with Youngin', titled 'Street Pain'. The entire club was drunk and vibing, but the Block Boyz remained militant while concealing their firearms, embracing the limelight in a very focused and humble manner.

"You know I thank all y'all for coming out to vibe wit' ya boy tonight. A special thanks to everybody who bought da album today 'cause y'all who I do it for. Before we get outta here, I wanna properly let y'all get acquainted with my nigga. My dawg coming from da bottom of da clip… yeah, dat 3-0-5! From his hood to my hood, we were represented," Danny Boi stated as Lyric stood in the background lighting a Cohiba cigar. He was certain Youngin' was about to follow suit and represent like Danny Boi had done.

Youngin' embraced the moment as he stood center stage, shouting enthusiastically, "Where my real niggas at in dis muthafucka?" He paused to allow the dawgs to get their bark on while throwing up their sets. "Now if you independent and you know you a badd bitch, let me know you in da building," Youngin' directed. Nearly every woman in the club shouted femininely, raising their manicured hands in sync.

"Dats what I'm talking 'bout. Dis single I'mma bless da streets with is called 'I Do it for Y'all', so ride wit' ya boy and put it in da air," Youngin' stated. The DJ dropped the beat on cue as if the two had been touring together and the moments were scripted. Youngin's words flowed like water as he rapped:

"To da hustlers on da grind, getting stacks totin' straps, let dem bustas know you livin' like dat... I do it for y'all, I do it for y'all, I do it for y'all, yep I do it for y'all... To all da ladies gettin' paper, got dese bustas goin' crazy, now you never got no time fa a hater... I do it fa y'all, I do fa y'all, I do it fa y'all, yep I do it fa y'all... Old school flava in da candy red 64', with a badd red bone and she stand 'bout 6'4... she a freak so I told her to bring six mo'... slow motion vibe so she only wanna lick slow... try to jack and from da glock, I'll let six go... if I miss I'll return da fire wit fo' mo'... Black gem, yeah da dude's a rare shiner... dunking backwards wit da rock, Harold Miner... on fire like da Heat, yeah I'm da light... hold court causin' havoc in da game, Bob Knight..."

Youngin' wowed the crowd as they certified his swag. Everyone in his entourage was amazed at his energizing performance. After it was over, the Dynamic Duo entourage crept out the back of the club, discreetly fleeing the club scene.

Chapter 26

"Shaun, where you at chic?"

"At da crib ova in Southwood, wassup?"

"I got something important I wanna holla at you 'bout, so meet me in 45 minutes if you can," Jamilah stated.

"Aight, give me a second. I'll be there and if I get lost I'll call you," Shaun replied. Following Jamilah's precise directions, Shaun was traveling northbound on Capital Circle N.E., riding on her black and red Yamaha motorcycle. Once she spotted Zaxby's restaurant just ahead, she signaled the right blinker and turned into the parking lot. Cutting off the ignition, Shaun rested her size 7, black Timberland construction boots that were loosely laced onto the steamy, late Summer asphalt.

Shaun removed the black helmet, shaking her silky, black hair free, then walked into the restaurant. As she was walking inside, dudes pumping gas at the adjacent Citgo store were in a trance due to the way Shaun was swaying her hips in the form-fitting blue DKNY denim jeans, with a tight, white wife-beater shirt that exposed her hard body. Shay waved her hand from a corner booth as Jamilah was at the counter purchasing three medium-sized sweet teas. They congregated and were ready to order.

"Wassup, girl?" Shay asked as Shaun was having a seat.

"Nothin' much. Just da usual."

"True, but girl I ain't know you ride."

"Yeah girl, I used to be a tomboy growing up, so da hustlers in my hood back in da day taught me how."

When Jamilah returned to the table, they all engaged in small talk until their bellies were full from the array of chicken delicacies that Zaxby's served.

"Well, I guess you wanna know why I asked you to come here. As you know, me and Shay some badd bitches and you cut from da same cloth. Anyway, I been keepin' my ear to da street and got word about dis lame ass white boy thinkin' he Black supplyin' da whole North Florida and South Georgia region with purp, kush, and hydro weed. He makin' a killin' worth, 'bout three hundred stacks or more. He out in Cairo, Georgia, growing it and since he got police on payroll, he think nobody can touch him." Jamilah whispered, loud enough for Shaun to hear.

"Say no mo, just let me kno when and I'm in," Shaun replied.

"Whateva we hit for, we split equally," Jamilah concluded.

"Dade County bitches 'bout bread, so believe me, ain't no pressure."

Two days later, Shay was strutting across the gravel walkway leading up to the doorway of the Cairo, Georgia, home. Two weeks prior, while performing her investigative duties, Shay followed the dude who called himself Red White to a local seafood market, manipulating an appealing way to introduce herself. Red White thought he was Black, so his ultimate weakness was a true ebony dimepiece that exemplified a cutout from Smooth Girl Magazine.

When Red White opened the door, he smiled with a platinum pull-out grill that was often boasted about. Supposedly Paul Wall from Houston, Texas, designed it for him.

"Wassup, sexy?" Shay stated, stroking his ego as she crossed the threshold of the front door.

"Right now, you wassup," Red White replied, attempting to go into mack mode. Being a master at deception, Shay concealed her true intentions like a black widow spider patiently waiting to strike.

"The other girls will be here in 'bout twenty minutes. I'mma go upstairs to get dressed in something I know you'll like," Shay stated in the tone of a harmless kitty kat, while simultaneously kissing Red White's cheek gently. He blushed like an eighth grader about to receive his first sexcapade. Twenty minutes later, a white van with the logo 'Exclusive Essence' written on the sides in pink letters pulled up as Jamilah and Shaun hopped out dressed in pink boy shorts and bras with white and pink leather stilettos and leather gloves.

While staring out the window, Red White got hard feeling as if his life had transformed into a porno movie. Shay told him that she had a treat for him, but two extra flawless black divas was more like a chocolate cake that he couldn't wait to eat. When Red White opened the door holding a bottle of Belvedere, Shaun instantly manipulated his ego.

"Damn daddy, Shay told us you were fine as hell, but even dat was an understatement." Red White just smiled, exposing all thirty-two teeth, feeling like a Don and unaware of what was about to happen. Jamilah came inside behind Shaun, toting a black Prada duffel bag with a couple straps tucked underneath clothing and scented body oils.

As they were sitting around downing a few drinks in their system to get the vibe right, Jamilah, the expert tactician stated, "Red White, how 'bout you get naked with us 'cause my pussy wet and I wanna see what you workin wit'." She wasn't intending to remove any clothing. Red White, being lame as he was, nearly ripped off his clothing and began to jack off. As much as his fake ass disgusted the three women, they all surrounded him for the future benefit. Shaun squatted down to half-heartedly massage his legs, praying he didn't prematurely cum on her while Jamilah tricked him into allowing her to cuff his hands in front of him. He was a freak, so he was down for that. As Shaun heard the clicking of the cuffs, she instantly shackled his ankles.

Red White thought to himself, "Damn dese black bitches some freaks," still transfixed in a naïve state of mind. Snapping him back to reality, Shay trailed her index finger down his pale, tattooed chest.

"You got to be dumbest cracka I've ever seen in my life, you know dat," she said. Instantly, Red White started crying, realizing that he was trapped in a defenseless position when Jamilah and Shaun both had chrome plated .9 mils pointed at each side of his cranium.

"Listen, we didn't come to kill you. We just want da money, but if you don't stop crying, you dead. Point blank," Shaun remarked calmly.

"Alright, everythang downstairs in the basement. Just don't shoot me please," Red White responded, sobbing as his natural, countrified accent manifested.

"Well come on, walk us down there. If you lying, we gon' kill you on the spot for thinking we a joke," Jamilah threatened, helping Red White to his feet as he waddled like a penguin leading the way. Down inside the basement, Red White neatly had five hundred pounds of hydro compressed and wrapped in weight of twenty-five pounds each. He also had two hundred pounds of kush compressed and wrapped by weight of the same, along with one hundred pounds of purp. Located inside a metal locker on the floor was approximately four hundred ten thousand dollars neatly stacked as if they were coming off the Federal Reserve Bank printing press. While Shay and Shaun loaded the van for the next forty-five minutes, Jamilah kept the pistols pointed to the back of Red White's head, allowing the cold steel to touch him.

"If you make a sound, I'mma splatter your thoughts all over dis dirty ass basement. Just be cool and you'll live to discuss this war story with ya kids!"

Once the task of loading the spoils of war into the van was complete, Shaun never spoke a word. She screwed the silencer onto the barrel of the pistol she toted and pumped two shots into Red White's temple, causing him to immediately slump over.

Shaun then stated, "There's no way he can live after seeing our face. Let's get outta here and don't leave nothing behind." They headed back upstairs. Little did they know, the package they just hit for belonged to a few officers in the area who arranged it for pickup. They were in for a rude awakening. Neither of the women actually cared about ruffling feathers though because there was a steep price to pay for those who put on the facade of so-called gangsters but were not trained for the lifestyle of constant pressure.

Once they made it back safely to Tallahassee, the girls pulled up to a rental home on Fred George Road that was rented under a fictitious name. It was used as a home base to count and split all profits. Everyone received one-hundred thirty five thousand dollars apiece, along with thirty-three pounds of purp to do as they pleased. They planned to drop the extra pound of purp to Lyric when they passed the studio on Tharpe Street and the remainder of the marijuana would be given as a gift to the Block Boyz to serve the streets, if the need arose.

Chapter 27

"Dang, I thought you got my number fa no reason 'cause you act like you ain't wanna call me."

"Naw, I just been a lil busy but I'm here now, right?" Will responded, stepping through the front entrance of a two-bedroom apartment in a complex called Campus Pointe.

"Yeah, you right. I'mma give you a pass 'cause I think you sexy," Makayla replied, smiling.

"I appreciate da compliment, but you da star of da show, ya dig."

"I can go for that. So what it do wit you?" Makayla asked.

"Just vibin' on da money trail." As Will was speaking, a five-foot-eleven pecan tan dimepiece came out the room wearing a T-shirt that had the word EPICUREAN embroidered across the front; a Florida A&M University modeling troupe.

"Will, this my roommate, Mickey. She from Birmingham, Alabama. Mickey, this Will," Makayla stated, introducing the two.

"How you doin', Will? Girl, you won't believe this broke ass nigga, John, on Facebook taking pictures with money all around him, talkin' 'bout number one hustler. He know damn well he just cashed his financial aid net check," Mickey stated, laughing uncontrollably.

"Yeah, he came to the Journalism building today wearing that big fake ass chain," Makayla chimed in.

"Dat boy ain't nothin' but a college thug. I'm a Barbie doll and my status is vital."

"Not to cut y'all off, but do y'all smoke?" Will asked.

"Not often, but right now I need to go up 'cause I have to figure out a way to get paid in dis college town," Mickey said.

"Yeah, you ain't lying. There ain't no jobs hiring and it's illegal to strip. I gotta get my books, plus pay the remainder of these out-of-state tuition costs, and financial aid ain't gonna be enough," Makayla responded with a somewhat frustrated demeanor.

"Aight, well I'mma roll up some of dis to ease ya mind and if y'all really 'bout making some extra money, I got a proposition for you," Will stated, pulling out a mid-size Ziploc bag stuffed with some of the dro Shaun dropped off in the Block Boyz life. Will got them higher than the State Capitol building once he realized the two of them would be his way into the college community. They needed help and he planned to utilize their services to push the weed without being seen, solely for the benefit of future provisions by college graduates whose resources he would always need in life.

***

"Yeah bruh, dis da area we call da Northside."

"It look like niggas ova here getting it," Youngin' replied.

"Oh yeah! Dis da infamous Basin Street, ya dig, and it's some real niggas ova here about dat," Danny Boi replied as he allowed the two-door, tinted window 2009 model Chevy Monte Carlo to coast through the streets on factory tires.

"You know me. I'm a street nigga, so I feel da need to ask about some street shit," Youngin' stated.

"Wassup? Talk to me," Danny Boi responded.

"What it's gon' take fa da Block Boyz to put work in da community, or in other words, who gotta get knocked off?"

"Now you speakin' my language. Da dude holdin' all da weight down long overdue. I really feel he had something to do with my partner getting killed at da Southside Flea Market. Only reason I ain't go preach to da nigga is 'cause at da time I was on trial for murda one, ya dig. Da nigga a busta!"

"Just give me da rundown on dude. Lil homie dem ready to ride," Youngin' responded.

"I got you, don't worry. I still got one of my partners dis way dat they gon' bless wit da work. But listen, we gotta show in fo' days at Club La

Vela in Panama City, so we'll take care of dat issue when we return. Relay word to everybody so we'll be moving in military fashion. Dis a real power move, so make sho' lil homies got they game faces on. I'mma introduce dem to a heavy hitter I know personally from my days having da streets in a headlock," Danny Boi stated.

"Ain't no pressure, 'cause dis da life we was built for," Youngin' replied before sparking up a blunt of purp, compliments of the ladies of Dynamic Duo Entertainment.

Chapter 28

Under the pitch black skyline, a Yukon Denali SUV Convoy wrapped in Danny Boi's album cover pierced through the Bay County limits, staying aware of any state troopers on Highway 231 Southbound. Danny Boi wasn't scheduled to perform until 12:30 a.m., so they all pulled over into the mall parking lot to congregate for a second. Lyric, Youngin', and Danny Boi were in the front of the truck. The three ladies trailed behind while the Block Boyz were in the last truck. After approximately fifteen minutes, they continued their trek down 23rd street, crossing the Hathaway Bridge to arrive at Club La Vela on Thomas Drive.

Upon seeing the energized crowd outside the club, Danny Boi turned his swag up to the max, realizing that his album's success was evident. The Dynamic Duo entourage crept through the back to alert the event promoter and hung out, smoking and drinking before Youngin' opened up the show for Danny Boi. As usual, the two front-running artists from the newly established label shut Panama City Beach down, bedazzling all in attendance.

Backstage, Shay, Jamilah, and Shaun were being persuaded by a young Jamaican woman in her early 20s to be featured in a magazine called FLAVAS, which was soon to be launched. In the midst of her briefing the women on the details of the magazine, she and Solo locked eyes and instantly embraced their mutual, sexual attraction. Once she set a future appointment to meet the women in Tallahassee, Solo approached her to place his bid.

"How you doing sexy?" Solo asked.

"I'm feelin' myself, movin' wit da clock always on my grind. How you?"

"Shit, I'm ridin' da same wave you on, but you stole my interest for a second, ya smell me. I'm Solo, and you?" He extended his right hand.

"You can call me Avia," she stated, returning the cordial greeting. Avia had a bright, reddish-yellow skin complexion with shoulder length dreads that were auburn colored at the tips. Her hazel-green eyes placed him in a trance, while her alluring smile revealed six open-face gold teeth on the bottom grill.

"So where you from?" Solo asked.

"Originally Portmore, Jamaica, but right now I got a crib in Fort Lauderdale. Honestly, I be everywhere."

"So what brought you to Panama City?"

"Danny Boi one of da hottest artists in da streets right now, so in order to find some badd bitches to model for my new magazine, I gotta follow who they chasin'," Avia replied.

"Dats some hustla shit, boo! How old are you, 'cause not many young women mind work like dat?"

"Boy, I ain't nothin' but twenty-fo."

"Oh okay, dats respect, rude gal. So when can I expect to see yo sexy ass in the mag?"

"Dats a surprise," Avia replied, smiling.

"Listen, Danny Boi, dats fam, as well as da women you were just talkin' to. I wanna vibe with you on a later date, so how 'bout you shoot me ya number."

"You can get dat, 'cause to be honest you very handsome, boo," Avia replied, rubbing her palm against Solo's freshly bald, shaved face. As Solo was locking Avia's phone number into his cellphone, Danny Boi approached from behind.

"Ay, Solo, come on lil bruh. I got someone you need to meet. Everybody waitin' on you."

"Aight, I'm comin' now," Solo replied.

"Hey before y'all leave, do you mind if I get a picture with y'all?" Avia asked.

"Anything for da people," Danny replied as Avia motioned for her photographer while she stood between the men.

"Will said he on his way ova here," Makayla stated, placing her cellphone on the granite countertop.

"Alright," Mickey replied. Twenty minutes later, Will was entering the apartment with a Louie bookbag thrown across his left shoulder as Speed followed behind with a bag also draped the same way.

"Wassup, ladies?" asked Will.

"You, of course," Makayla replied, flirtatiously.

"Everything kosher," Mickey stated.

"By da way, dis my brother, Speed. Mickey, I brought him here for you 'cause you told me you was searching for da real," Will said.

"What they do, cutie?" Speed asked, flashing his panty-wetting smile.

"Whateva yo fine ass want me to do," Mickey responded.

"I want you to make money while you handle ya business in school. You bout dat?"

"I wouldn't have it no other way," Mickey replied.

"If dats da case, me and bruh gone be y'all tutors for Hustlenomics 101," Speed remarked, having a seat at the square, wooden table in the dining room.

For the next two hours, Makayla and Mickey bagged up two pounds of dro upon instructions given via Will and Speed. Once everything was appropriately stashed, Will pulled out a bottle of

Patron, welcoming Mickey and Makayla to the finer things in life as they all began swallowing shots.

When Makayla swallowed her second shot of liquor, she voiced her true feelings. "Will, I wanna fuck you right now."

He nodded his head, never saying a word, then swallowed a shot of Patron. Mickey, being the freak she was, verbally offered her desires as well.

"Speed, I want you to beat dis pretty pussy from da back and then I want you to put my legs on your neck and fuck me good!" On cue, the next two hours were filled with blissful screaming and moaning as two-thirds of the Block Boyz laid the tongue and dick game down Dade County style, as if Trick Daddy or Uncle Luke schooled them personally.

"Listen, tomorrow y'all gone crank up, so go ahead and relax and get ya mind right. Spread da word on da low, but neva ova da phone. Shop doesn't open til 5:30 p.m. every day. Dats when we gon' be here for protection purposes, ya dig."

"Don't worry, Will. We gon' handle dat 'cause dese lame ass dudes gon' be rushing to give us they money," Makayla replied.

"Fasho, we gon' holla back in a few," Will responded before he and Speed left the apartment.

Once they were in the car, Speed spoke from the driver seat while rolling a Backwood. "Dat boy

Solo texted me. He at da spot waitin' on us. We got 'bout two hours before we open the trap."

"Aight, stop by dat Circle K on da way to da house so I can grab a few of dem energy drinks," Will responded.

"Yeah, I got you, but shit dis herb gon' power me up, ya dig," Speed stated, pulling the Cadillac CTS out of the complex, making a left onto South Adams Street.

Chapter 29

The reflection in the full-body, tri-fold mirror was that of a Black woman scorned seeking revenge on anybody in the way. Casually draped in a navy blue wife beater, a pair of tight-fitting denim blue jeans, some navy blue and white Adidas and a New York Yankees fitted cap, Rain was applying makeup to her face, attempting to bring life to her cocaine-cratered skin. Despite the downward spiral of her health condition, she was still a tasty eyeful to those who couldn't pierce the veil of her venomous black eyes.

Once she finished powdering her face, Rain took a deep breath, beginning her journey downstairs to an altered reality of a new life for herself. All baggage not needed was left within the confines of the vacant apartment, along with the tri-fold mirror.

The time was approximately 3:00 a.m., as the full moon illuminated the horizon while the navy blue Range Rover with 24-inch chrome DUB floaters glided gracefully on the highway. After catching a glimpse of Danny Boi's video on BET's 106 & Park, she decided it was time to travel north to Tallahassee in hopes of meeting him for a second time, with intentions of seizing the opportunity given. If she was a woman of intellect, the mission would have been aborted, but instead she loaded the SUV to capacity with designer luggage and took off.

While inside the car, Rain swallowed her H.I.V. medication, taking a long gulp of water from the Zephyrhills squirt bottle. She fired up a wine-flavored Black & Mild and focused her energy on completing her journey up Florida's Turnpike, northbound, speeding in an attempt to bypass the early morning rush-hour traffic.

"Da fat bastard come out at da same time every night. In three minutes, Speed, start da car. Me and Will gone light his ass up soon as he sit in his car," Solo instructed.

"Fifty fo," Speed replied. On cue, following his daily routine, the Northside Tallahassee Kingpin stood on the front porch of the trap house. After checking his wristwatch as usual, the kingpin known as Caine took his normal eight steps and sat in his Mercedes ML430 AMG truck. Once he lit the Newport short cigarette and inhaled the nicotine, he never had an opportunity to exhale in peace. The next ten seconds were as if an alarm clock rang out in the streets before dawn.

Will and Solo stood side by side in front of the truck, both empting nearly half a clip through the glass windshield. Caine's body was riddled with so many shells that it caused him to lay slumped on the steering wheel, resembling an old, raggedy Cabbage Patch doll. The two masked men backed away from the scene with AK-47s pointed towards surrounding houses, ready to rip fire at any potential witness. They slid into the car like an experienced assassins' team, driving away unseen.

Once they arrived at their mini-penthouse, the decision was made to keep their trap closed for the day. Two hours later, Youngin' arrived after hearing the details of the homicide via the local WCTV news channel on television.

"Everythang taken care of, big homie," Speed stated, dapping Youngin' as he entered the house.

"You know soundwaves travel fast and far in dese parts, ya smell me. What's understood need not be explained," Youngin' replied.

"Nuff said. Respect, badmon!" Youngin' stated, pausing before continuing. "So wassup wit y'all boyz fa da day?"

"You kno I'm wit' whateva. I don't know 'bout dem boyz, but they upstairs playin' Madden on da PS3. Holla at 'em," Speed replied. Youngin' entered the loft area, greeted first by the intoxicating smell of marijuana.

"What they do fam?"

"You know, reppin' fa da Dade every day," Will replied, standing up to salute the general.

"Five alive daily, you know," Solo stated, greeting him the same.

"Respect! Ay, I want y'all boyz to bomb thru da studio a lil bit and vibe wit' da fam," Youngin' stated.

Everyone agreed to hang out in the studio and began to freshen up before taking off. At approximately 10:00 a.m., the four of them arrived. Speed stepped out the Range Rover with Youngin' and Solo, backing his CTS in the lot, with Will exiting from the passenger side. Lyric and Danny Boi were inside hard at work, as usual, attempting to manifest classic music. Lately, Youngin' had adopted the same work ethic upon the realization that he was blessed with a musical gift.

Four hours had passed and many possible chart-topping songs were created, then stored into the vault for future play. Speed inspired Solo and Will to get a taste for the mic when he stepped in the booth and freestyled to perfection, actually shocking himself. While they were hanging out witnessing Youngin' do his thing, Speed received a call on his cellphone. He placed his cup of Ciroc Vodka mixed with pineapple juice down and answered the caller. Twenty minutes later, Mickey was outside in the parking lot, waiting on Speed to come out.

"Ay, I'mma catch y'all in a lil bit. I'm 'bout to slide wit' dis broad fa a minute," Speed stated, walking around the studio dapping everybody.

"You strapped, right?" Danny Boi asked, aware that the Leon County streets played foul at times.

"Er'day, you already know."

"Aight, before you go, take ya share of da bread for taking care of dat bizz," Danny Boi stated, passing him, as well as Will and Solo, twenty stacks of neatly wrapped rubberbands apiece.

Speed received his unexpected cut and stuffed it in his back, deep-pocket, stonewashed Sean John denim jeans. When he stepped outside into the midday sunlight, the crispy V-neck white T-shirt gave the sun its only competition, it seemed.

"What's hood witcha, boo?" Speed asked, sitting in the passenger seat of the white, tinted-window Chevy Camaro, 2010 edition.

"Just came from dis Black Psychology class on campus getting it in," Mickey replied, as Speed noticed the college books on the backseat.

"Dats what it is. So what you 'bout to get into?"

"Well I got a few people that want to spend some money, so I wanted to see if you would come hold me down while I handle dat," Mickey replied.

"Yeah, I'll take care of dat, but stop somewhere so I can get somethin' to eat."

"Aight, bae," Mickey replied, totally unaware that Speed was contemplating putting her car on upgrade status.

Chapter 30

"Dang son, I thought you forgot I was up here."

"Naw, dat afternoon traffic serious up dis way, but what you got a sweet tooth or something?" Youngin' asked.

"I seen dat 'Now Hot' sign come on so I had to get me a dozen," Pops replied, toting a box of Krispy Kreme glazed donuts.

"Hell, let me get one," Youngin' stated, opening the box.

Sitting in the blue Range Rover in the adjacent Circle K gas station parking lot located on North Monroe street, Rain was using a quarter to scratch off the numerous lottery tickets she had just bought to basically test her luck. Upon raising her head briefly to take a sip of the Coca-Cola flavored ICEE, it was like hitting a million dollar scratch ticket. She noticed Youngin', despite him trying to conceal his countenance with a vintage Miami Heat fitted cap.

"Finally the break I needed," Rain whispered to herself, prepared to follow him to his whereabouts as her stakeout began.

"Ay Pops, follow me so you can drop the trailer off at the shop I got for you."

"Aight, lead the way," Pops replied. Youngin' needed his dad in town to paint a few automobiles, so he rented out a garage on monthly payments. Pops could pick up and leave at any time if circumstances called for it.

Unbeknownst to him, Youngin' was being watched from a distance by Rain who was certain that he'd eventually lead her to the man of interest, Danny Boi. Since Danny Boi and Youngin' instructed the little homies not to open up shop until they gave the word, Will and Speed had been posted up with Mickey and Makayla for the time being, flooding the streets with weed and helping the two hard-working college girls get their currency up.

"What got you looking stressed out like dat?" Will asked.

"Well I gotta get this dissertation done for class before homecoming week," Makayla replied.

"Oh yeah, what's it about?"

"I'm preparing an in-depth presentation about the Nation of Islam and how it shaped Black America in the 1930s. I'm not really stressed. I just like perfection you know, plus Minister Farrakhan is such a positive figure for our people right now that I'm careful not to misrepresent the movement."

"I'm no student, but I did read a book once when I was young called *Message to the Black Man*. It was very deep too," Will responded.

"Yeah, the Most Honorable Elijah Muhammad wrote that!" Makayla replied excitedly.

"I can't wait to hear your presentation. Anyways, what's up with this Homecoming issue? I've been hearing a lot about it," Will asked, lighting a blunt as Speed and Mickey entered the apartment toting four white Styrofoam plates from G & G's Jamaican diner.

"Dis fa all bruh," Speed stated, causing Makayla to take a break from the laptop computer because her brain was craving supplements.

"Fasho. Well since we all here can anybody break me off 'bout dese Homecoming events?" Will asked pretending to be dumbfounded as he was already up to par with the events.

"It's gonna be so much going on, but the most happenin' event gon' be da concert. So many people gon' be in town and I wouldn't mind seeing Danny Boi and the other guy Youngin' he got the song with 'cause that song is actually on my MySpace intro right now. They hot!" Mickey stated enthusiastically.

"Oh yeah?" Will replied, laughing at these up-incoming ladies.

"By da way, we gon' be in the fashion show so y'all come support us," Makayla stated, shocking Will because she never mentioned she modeled.

"So y'all doing it big bruh?" Speed asked.

"Trying to, but I can't wait to stunt on dese broads when I get some rims for my whip tho," Mickey responded.

"As a matter of fact, I got some black 23s I took off my whip. We'll get 'em put on today," Speed stated as the Block Boyz were already in preparation for Homecoming.

"Shit girl, you talking about rims. I gotta get rid of da Jetta first," Makayla remarked, taking a bite of her brown-stewed chicken and rice meal.

"If you wanted a new car all you had to do was ask," Will stated, pausing for a second while dialing a number on his cellphone.

"What they do big homie? You still got some people at da lot? Aight tell dem I'll be through there in an hour," Will spoke before hanging up the cell. "Once we finish eating we'll go handle dat," Will said to Makayla who was in shock.

"I'mma take Mickey to holla at Pops," Speed informed with intentions to surprise her with a paint job also.

"Yeah, they been grinding hard so they deserve it," Will remarked, exposing who he was with, shocking the ladies. Speed started laughing, simultaneously exposing his chain. Speed and Will pre-arranged the occasion because before this moment they never wore their jewelry to the girls' apartment.

"Oh yeah before I forget, we were supposed to find some models for an upcoming magazine and we chose y'all two if y'all wit dat," Speed filled them in.

Mickey and Makayla glanced at each other matter of factly then shouted in unison, "Hell yeah!" while high fiving each other.

"Aight well da photo shoot gonna be in a couple days so be prepared to be sitting in the hair salon tomorrow. By da way, da magazine go on sale Homecoming week so of course it's gonna boost y'all status out here. Always remember we scratch your back so if we ever need you, do the same."

"It's not a problem," Mickey replied.

Chapter 31

"Uh-huh... I think this her right here, I'll call you back," Shaun stated before hanging up the phone. Walking up to the young lady in the yellow BCBG form-fitting T-shirt with blue denim hip huggers covering her perfectly formed assets, she approached her with, "Hey, how you doin', you Egypt, right?" She extended a gentle, freshly manicured hand.

"Yeah that's me and you are?"

"No need to be startled cutie, I've been sent here to scoop you up. You waitin' on Youngin', right?"

"Yes I am. Sorry I didn't mean to seem disrespectful or anything. I'm just up here and ain't nothing goin' right. I'm thinkin' 'bout quitting school and going back home," Egypt replied.

"Just chill, you gon' be alright. But come on, we got people waiting on us," Shaun said, turning around leading the way to a white-on-white Porsche Cayenne with recently bought five percent tinted windows. Once they sat inside the SUV, Shaun placed a call to Youngin' on speakerphone in order to ease Egypt's state of mind.

"Listen, before we link up with Youngin' we gon' make a few stops."

"Aight, dats cool," Egypt replied as Shaun began driving down Magnolia Drive and cranked the radio up a few notches. Ten minutes later, they arrived at a unisex barber and beauty shop called Clippers located on South Adams Street, adjacent to the Florida A&M University campus.

"Retta, dis my girl Egypt right here and I need you to get her all dolled up. Can you handle dat?" Shaun asked, already knowing the response.

"Girl, I'm sure Shay and Jamilah done told you about me," Retta responded jokingly.

"Yeah girl, I know you da best in da business so my people in good hands like Allstate."

"Please believe it!" Retta stated, handing Egypt a style book to look through.

"Alright, I'll be back in a few." Shaun walked back through the gawking stares of the barbers and patrons, exiting the building. Upon sitting her juicy ass back on the plush, white leather interior, Shaun pulled out a freshly rolled blunt from the glove compartment, inhaled a good puff then called Youngin' again. "Where you at? ... Aight, I'm right 'round the corner, I'm coming." Danny Boi, Will, Speed, Solo and Youngin' were secluded on the side of the paint & body car garage that Pops was working out of, having a male bonding session. Interrupting the moment, Shaun entered the cypher, smelling and looking very feminine.

"What's good fellas?"

"Hell, right now the streets and the ladies lovin' da big homie Danny Boi," Speed responded.

"Yeah, dese college bitches ready to see you in concert come to think of it," Shaun confirmed with a smile.

"I'mma give 'em a good one too," Danny Boi replied, slapping five with Youngin' to his right then Solo to his left.

"So wassup, where Egypt?" Youngin' asked.

"Ova at Clippers getting her hair done."

"She know 'bout da photo shoot tomorrow?" Youngin' asked.

"Damn come to think of it, I left two broads up there," Will cut in.

"They up under the dryer. They 'bout done, but uh naw I ain't tell her yet," Shaun responded.

"It's straight, we'll tell her later tonight," Youngin' replied.

"Ay Speed, you ridin wit me?" Will asked.

"Yeah."

"Damn dem broads ain't got no car?" Shaun asked.

"Yeah, but Pops blessin' 'em wit a lil paint job so in da meantime da kid playing da chauffeur role, ya smell me," Will replied, smiling cunningly.

"Unh huh. If I know my lil brothers like I do, I know y'all up to something," Shaun remarked.

"What's understood need not be explained," Speed stated before sliding into the passenger seat of the rental car.

"Shit, to think of it, Avia and her cameraman gon' be at da airport at three. I'm 'bout to go ahead and take care of dat." Solo headed over to Youngin's Range Rover because Pops was also hooking up the cars the Block Boyz owned.

"Well Danny Boi you and Youngin' wanna smoke sum of dis purp before I go back and scoop Egypt?"

"Yeah, let's smoke in da car tho," Danny Boi replied, conscious of his surroundings. As if being on a secret espionage venture for the past ten minutes scoping out the scenery from behind her tinted windows, Rain sat silently, bird watching.

Upon seeing Danny Boi attempting to conceal his image and Youngin's sexy ass following, she smiled until she spotted a sore sight for the eyes and shouted, "Oh hell fuck naw, I'mma kill dat bitch!" She continued to sit and stare despite her inability to see through the windows. Once everyone dispersed, Rain figured that was her cue to attempt to get Pops within her poisonous grasp. The mission failed because Pops locked himself in the garage alone with his work and one of his favorite Keith Sweat CDs, unable to hear the knocking on the door. As Rain was headed back to her car, Will just so happened to be riding back by, noticing a familiar face… silently promising to tell Shaun he'd seen the girl that used to come through the block in Miami to pick her up when they were trapping in the Back Blues off 135th Street.

Chapter 32

"On time fellas. That's a rare excellent attribute to possess, especially with his new breed of hustlers."

"We come from a breed of old-school gangstas so da game was given to us properly," Solo stated, extending his right hand.

"That's real. Well have a seat and order some breakfast on me before you head back," Smiley stated.

Smiley was a forty-four year old mixed breed of Peruvian, Cherokee Indian and Black descent. This old-school veteran had been one of the largest cocaine suppliers traveling across the border for the last twenty years. He originally met the three Block Boyz the night Danny Boi introduced them and today was the morning of their first business mission. The four of them were gathered at a table near the side restaurant window of Applebee's with a transparent view of everything taking place outside. Smiley instructed them on everything while they ate.

"Outside, there are two Jeep Cherokees, one champagne and the other silver. Everything is stashed at the bottom of the floors as I'm sure Danny Boi instructed you on how to get it out. You see those two white girls in the Lexus truck, yeah as fine as they appear to be, dem bitches dangerous. Well anyway, one of y'all go out and drop the money bags in the car with them and whoever driving the Cherokees go start them and get comfortable before you take off. Remember, every two months we'll meet in different spots and you'll always bring the jeeps back as I'll have two more just alike," Smiley instructed as Speed stood up to go outside and transfer the money bags. "One more thing. If y'all ever need an issue cleaned up, don't ever hesitate to call," Smiley spoke assuring them that the street marriage they were in was set in stone.

"Fasho," Will replied, shaking his hand before relieving himself in one of the restaurant's urinals.

When Will came out of the restaurant, Speed was waiting in the rental while Solo was anticipating the one-hour journey waiting in the champagne-colored Cherokee, leaving the silver one to him. Once Will plopped down inside and adjusted to the seats, he said a silent prayer to the hustler's god and they all took off, careful not to make a mistake.

The Lexus truck pulled out of the parking lot and shortly after Smiley was in the backseat puffing a blunt of dro while saluting himself for the cunning thought of his trademark, Peruvian cocaine moved in Cherokee automobiles. After a long day of working hard in the studio, Youngin' decided to discreetly go to The Moon nightclub. He entered through the side door about thirty minutes before the partygoers began to crowd the lines. Youngin' had the appearance of a plain Jane as he was draped in a white T-shirt, some black Rocawear jeans, a pair of black & grey Nike Air Raids and a New Era Oakland Raiders fitted cap with the brim low, attempting to conceal his image.

Youngin' positioned himself to the top level of the club at a table, attaining a bird's eye view with a pitcher of ice and a medium-sized pitcher of Long Island Iced Tea. Outside, the club immediately transfixed into an ambiance that resembled the BET Awards as everyone was on their star-like, hater-blocker vibe. Despite many having tunnel vision, they couldn't resist the temptation to turn their heads as Shay and Jamilah were arriving at the club whipping Danny Boi's purple 1975 Chevy Vert with 26-inch floaters. They were also bamming the hit song Danny Boi had on his album with Youngin'.

Anyone who understands badd bitches knows that they come by the flock, which was proven true as Mickey trailed behind in her newly painted purple Camaro on 23 inches. Makayla followed her in a purple Dodge Challenger on 23s as Avia was riding shotgun with her. The final car of the fleet was the white Porsche Cayenne driven by Shaun, with Egypt in the passenger seat. Lyric had already called the club owner who was a good friend of his, so when the ladies arrived it was as the red carpet was rolled out specifically for them. Immediately upon going in, Supastar Jay Kwik the Philly Dynamite was giving them the shout-outs, as well as announcing the release date of the magazine. Despite hearing his people were in the building, Youngin' remained incognito to everyone, with a minor exception. At first glance, she almost missed him but her blurred vision cleared up quickly under the clubs lights.

"Excuse me, how you doin'?" Youngin' initially wasn't going to respond, but he differed in his decision after noticing how fine she was.

"I'm good, just vibin. How are you and what's ya name?"

"Oh I'm sorry Youngin', my name is Retta and yeah I'm just vibin' myself 'cause I don't really get out much."

"So I guess me not tryin' to be seen ain't really workin' huh?" Youngin' replied smiling.

"Naw you good 'cause I had to look very close to make sho' that it was you. I been dying to meet you since da first time you and Danny Boi had a show here," Retta stated.

"Dats wassup. So how can I reach you if I need you?" Youngin' asked.

"Here, take my business card and on the back I'll put my cellphone number on there just for you," Retta responded.

"Aight, dats a bet. Well how long you gonna be in here 'cause I wanna leave wit you?"

"Oh I'm in here with my friend. I didn't even drive, so whenever she ready to go."

"Dats even better 'cause now you gon' be my designated driver," Youngin' replied laughing.

"Aight, but I'mma take you to my house. Just let me know when you ready."

"In a lil bit... uh, you and ya girl come vibe wit me," Youngin' stated as Supastar Jay Kwik began shouting over the mic.

"Where my ladies at who know they bad! ... Dats what I'm talkin' 'bout! This is an exclusive I'm 'bout to drop and I'm da only one got it 'cause my nigga just dropped it today, so if you got money and it's yours, show dat shit!" Supastar Jay Kwik directed, then crunk the club back up dropping an unreleased track from Youngin's upcoming debut album titled 'Flo Motion'. Witnessing the reaction of the people, Youngin' instantly knew he had a hit because the DJ pulled the track up and ran it from the top again.

When Youngin' finished that song earlier in the day, Lyric had emailed it to Supastar Jay Kwik anticipating it to become a part of his rotation, and for a small fee, it was. Less than fifteen minutes later, Youngin' and Retta were creeping out the side of the club as he gave her the keys to the Range Rover while he reclined the passenger seat. Wherever they were headed, Youngin' refused to worry because of course he was strapped like seatbelts, unafraid to slang iron if necessary.

Chapter 33

"I'm on da way now," Youngin' stated into the speakerphone while swerving lane to lane, sipping a Red Bull energy drink. Twenty minutes later, Youngin' was walking through the Southwood townhouse that the Block Boyz resided in.

"What's hood wit you?" Danny Boi asked while schooling Solo on the pool table.

"Everythang Dynamic Duo E.N.T got they hands in," Youngin' replied while walking around dapping everybody present.

"Well since we all here, let's get down to business," Danny Boi said as he placed the pool stick down on the table. Once everybody had a seat on the round sofa, Danny Boi continued, "As you know, the lil homies made a real power move. Moving it will not be a problem 'cause I already lined up my old customers for y'all in Bainbridge, Valdosta, Quincy, Gainesville, Jacksonville and of course my peeps on the Northside right here in da Capital City. Me and Youngin' gon' fall back and continue blazin' dis music shit. Believe me da streets gonna get real hot, but long as y'all stay low to the turf, everything will be smooth."

"So all dese peeps coming from outta town to shop?" Will asked.

"Yeah, except dem niggas in J-ville. Y'all faces certified so ain't nothin' to worry 'bout, but it's y'all decision to hit da road or not," Danny Boi replied.

"Ain't no pressure, but I hope they know it's gonna be a luxury tax on each pack we bring," Will remarked as Speed and Solo nodded in agreement.

"Dats y'all call. Me and Youngin' just the invisible enforcers in case shit ever need to get funky out here."

"Just know when we bust dis cash down y'all included, so fall back like O.G.'s do and watch our backs."

"We got y'all, so get ya grind on," Youngin' replied.

"Now dat everybody on da same page, I'm 'bout to hit da studio. By da way, Youngin', Lyric waiting on you 'cause he got some more tracks sampled that he feels will fit good on ya album if you blaze 'em right."

"Aight, let me make a stop by da spot and switch up my gear real quick," Youngin' replied.

"Oh yeah, before I go, here's a list of numbers for y'all to hit up. Niggas waitin' to place orders 'cause ain't really no work out here," Danny Boi stated.

"Aight, we on dat," Solo replied, altering his mindstate to grind mode, preparing to re-open the trap they established on the Southside of Tallahassee.

***

"You know I hate to come down here unexpectedly, but you acting like you don't wanna pay me."

"No it's not like dat, just give me a little more time please."

"I been giving you time and I really needs mine, Retta."

"Listen, I just met a major player in dis rap game named Youngin'. When I rob him, which should be soon, I'll have your money, plus interest," Retta replied.

"Aight, I'll give you ninety days, but the next time I have to drive down here from Atlanta, you know da consequences."

"Cash, I promise I'll have what I owe, plus I'm paying for my sister also so she don't have to sell her body for you no more," Retta stated.

"I hope so 'cause I'll hate to have to kill you," Cash replied.

"Aight, I'll see you in ninety." Retta reassured him and removed herself from the passenger seat of the Buick Lacrosse.

"Damn, I miss getting that pussy but my cash is what I live for," Cash said to himself as he watched Retta strut to the sliding glass door of the Lake Ella plaza Publix grocery store, as if she really had something to buy from within. Cash smoothed out the brim of his vintage Kangol fedora hat before exiting the parking lot and headed back to Georgia. In order to make the trek back, he needed gas, so he made a pit stop at the Circle K on North Monroe Street. Cash went inside to purchase a 44-ounce cup of grape soda. He also bought a box of Black & Mild cigars while paying for a gas fill-up. On the way out the door, he was halted by the voice of a gorgeous lady.

"Damn you lookin fly daddy."

"I appreciate da compliment, but I must be honest with you. My time doesn't come cheap so if that offends you, I must keep it moving," Cash replied.

"I'm actually a connoisseur of handsome men and trust me, money is not a factor when I see something I'd like to taste," Rain stated.

"Well if dats the case, I can postpone my trip home as long as your pockets are big as your mouth."

Rain thought to herself, "I know dis muthafucka ain't say dat shit!" but chose to conceal her motives. "Name your price?"

"Ten grand for an hour," Cash replied arrogantly.

"Alright, when you pump your gas follow me up the street to the Holiday Inn."

Less than twenty minutes later, Rain and Cash were naked in room 515 exploring each other's bodies. Before they even started, Rain paid him fifteen grand instead of ten. Cash was so focused on pleasing his customer that he got lost in the moment traveling amidst her curvaceous body that he never put on a condom. Rain's intentions had been satisfied as another victim would soon understand her agony of dying slowly. An hour later, Cash left his number on the counter for her to call any time she needed a fix. If he only knew the web he was caught in, Cash would have killed Rain on the spot.

Chapter 34

"For everybody who missed da Homecoming concert last night, I'll be da first one to tell you it was off da chain. Da kid Youngin' did his thang and if you listenin' big homie, the fans been calling all day showin' love. Da streets been screamin' for you to stop thru da Blazin 102.3 studios..." Shaun tuned in and listened to DJ 1-Champ as she headed to FAMU's multi-purpose center in support of Makayla and Mickey's fashion show appearance. When she arrived in the parking lot, two candy-painted Cadillac CTS automobiles grabbed her attention. One was orange with matching 23-inch rims and the other one was identical, except it was fire red. Shaun was even more shocked to see Will and Speed passing out FLAVAS magazine free of charge in support of the ladies' movement. They actually purchased two boxes themselves in an attempt to help Avia and the rest of the women gain more exposure.

"What they do sis?" Speed asked as Shaun approached them.

"Bout to go in here and check out the show. Y'all coming with me?"

"Yeah we in there," Will replied as he and Speed left their guns in the car and activated the alarm system. Later that evening, Solo along with Avia met Makayla, Mickey, Will, and Speed at CHUBBY'S nightclub for the fashion show after the party. Shaun chose not to attend and, instead, decided to get a bite to eat from the Waffle House within walking distance of the club.

While sitting inside enjoying a midnight breakfast, Shaun had no idea that Rain was headed to the club seeking someone to silently victimize. Rain's plans to enter were altered after she spotted her second worst enemy, other than the virus she carried. The nightclub was so crowded that Rain's vehicle was parked on the adjacent side of the street near the Subway franchise. When Shaun drove off in the Porsche, she had no idea that someone was in hot pursuit of her. After making a few right turns then a couple left turns, Shaun peered into the rearview mirror.

"So you muthafuckas wanna follow me, huh?" she said aloud to herself as the navy blue Range Rover had come too close for comfort. Rain was too inexperienced to be trailing a gangstress of Shaun's caliber. Remaining calm, Shaun typed in the studio address on the vehicle's GPS device, simultaneously placing her .30 pistol in her lap and continuing to drive as if nothing was wrong.

"Youngin', you at the studio bae?" Shaun asked.

"Yeah, wassup?"

"I'm 'bout to slide thru because somebody think they gotta sweet lick and wanna follow me."

"Aight, I got chu," Youngin' concluded, ending the call. Rain realized her cover was blown and chose not to make the left turn behind Shaun when she spotted Youngin' standing outside smoking a Newport cigarette. His other hand was concealed in his pocket with his index finger rested atop his pistol's trigger. Rain continued to drive westbound and made a left turn at the following stop light.

Once she came to the intersection of High Road and Tennessee Street, she said to herself, "Damn I'm right back where I started," as she spotted the nightclub directly in front of her. "Fuck it, I might as well go in now. I'll catch dat bitch later!" She drove near the front and parked next to a yellow Delta '88 automobile.

When Rain entered the club, the hairs cemented within her pores stood at attention as the nightlife environment sent a surge of energy through her body, due to the fact that this was a comfort zone in a world all too familiar to her. The way DJ Demp spun records while allowing all the college partygoers to rep their cities kept the vibe so positive that the hustlers with a few dollars didn't mind keeping the bottles popping. As the night grew young, the patrons became drunk and unaware of their clothes.

"Ay ain't dat da broad who use to come thru da trap and scoop sis up sometimes?" Will asked Speed who was standing near with a personal bottle of Remy in his hand.

He focused in for a second then stated, "Hell yeah! Dat bitch in here shonin' wit dese young niggas."

"I'mma tell sis I seen her up here," Will replied. Avia was standing nearby tipsy as hell, anticipating Solo to hit her off after the club with the good sex game. As if his prayers were answered, a drunk college student recognized Avia from the FLAVAS magazine cover and was adamant about getting his feel on. Shocking Avia, dude palmed her ass under the sundress she was wearing while staring at Solo who was standing near with a unit on his face that said, "Yeah I did it and what fuck nigga!" Solo's first reaction was to overlook it, but he thought otherwise, refusing to live with the tormenting feeling of being tried.

"A-vee, take da keys and head out to da whip," Solo whispered while watching a dude named Derek nonchalantly walk towards the bathroom. As Solo walked off, Avia relayed the message to everyone else, but by this time Solo was already prepared to pounce on his prey. When he entered the bathroom, Derek was standing at the urinal taking a piss. Solo stepped behind him and mashed his face into the tile wall, breaking his nose. Derek was so much in shock that he turned around and pissed on Solo.

"You pussy muthafucka!" were Solo's last words before expertly spitting the razorblade out his mouth and slicing Derek down the side of his face. Blood gushed everywhere. Solo vanished from the scene, quickly dashing for the exit as the rest of his entourage made their exit as well.

"Ahhh, help me!" Derek yelled, stumbling out of the bathroom holding his bloodstained face while his pants were continually falling below his knees. Will and Speed already knew the craftsmanship of their partner as they watched him fall down on the floor. Refusing to be good Samaritans, they ushered the ladies out the door speedily, knowing Solo was already outside ready to flee. After seeing all the blood, it was pandemonium as everyone was attempting to get outside, refusing to be part of the aftermath. In the midst of the chaos, Will caught a glimpse of Rain fleeing to the blue Range Rover and stored the image into his mental rolodex.

Chapter 35

"Hello! Who in the world is calling me at four o'clock in da morning? It better be good 'cause I got an exam in four hours that I been resting my brain for," Egypt stated in a groggy voice.

Clearing his throat, the caller replied, "E, babygirl don't hang up… it's me, Jamal."

"You got some nerve. I haven't heard from you in ova a year and now you pop up out the blue. What in da hell could you possibly want?"

"I really need to see you about something very important. Please agree to see me because you are the only person I can trust," Jamal begged.

"I'm no longer in Miami. I'm in grad school in Tallahassee now."

"That's perfect! I'll be up there in two days and trust me, it'll be worth your time. I'll explain everything when I see you."

"Aight, but under one condition. Do not attempt to touch me."

"No problem. I'll call you when I reach town and thank you so much." Jamal stated, concluding the call.

The unexpected call caused Egypt's equilibrium to become unbalanced because she was wrestling the past emotions. Jamal proposed to her, then three days later he mysteriously vanished for nearly a year. Now, she was wondering about his motive for calling. Unable to go back to sleep, Egypt brewed a pot of coffee and began to study for the mid-term exam. She was forever thankful to Youngin' who paid her tuition, as well as the remainder of her apartment expenses, which allowed her the opportunity to be stress free in the process of obtaining a Master's.

***

Once the Block Boyz shut down operations for the day, they stashed the profits then went to the studio to hang with the rest of the Dynamic Duo family. Everyone was just hanging out, except Lyric, Youngin' and Danny Boi. They were hard at work, despite making it look simple.

"Sis, bruh told me 'bout dem muthafuckas following you da otha night," Will stated.

"Hell yeah! Shit was about to go bad for them tho cause I stay on point," Shaun replied.

"Dats real. Shit got bloody at da club dat same night. By da way, I know what I been wanting to tell you." Will paused.

Shaun then stated, "What is it lil bruh?"

"I seen dat chic who used to bom' thru da spot in Dade every now and then to scoop you up."

"Real shit!?"

"Hell yeah, she was whipping a navy blue Range Rover. Matter of fact, da broad was in da club da otha night."

"Oh shit, dat bitch was da one following me!"

"At least it was somebody you know," Will replied.

"Yeah, but I almost killed that bitch before we left da crib so I know she wanna X me out," Shaun said.

"So dat means we go into attack mode and apply a lil pressure, right?" Will asked.

"You already kno, but fuck dat bitch. I'mma smoke one on her ass," Shaun threatened.

"Fasho."

"Hey y'all, Danny Boi and Youngin's video done made it up to number two on 106 & Park. They 'bout to show it now," Jamilah stated with excitement, causing everyone to stand in front of the flat screen T.V. in support of the family.

Chapter 36

"I'm glad you chose to meet me here," Jamal stated as he took a seat at the table located on the inside of Borders bookstore.

"You seemed to be desperate, so I'm curious to know wassup," Egypt replied.

"First of all, the only reason I disappeared is because I was promoted to the undercover narcotics force and I refused to ever have you in danger because of the profession I chose. I understand there's not an adequate excuse, but I love you so much and refused to allow one of those gangsters down bottom to use you as a pawn to get to me. I hope that clears the tension between us. As far as why I contacted you, it is something that is very confidential. If I involve you, can you remain silent?"

"I'm here right," Egypt replied sarcastically.

"Okay, listen. Of course I've been placing my life in jeopardy for the force for the last year, but unfortunately I'm broke and underappreciated. Lately I've been piecing together a very important case in which I'm the only one with key information. Instead of placing these criminals behind bars, I believe them being free is more lucrative for me and you. I've formulated a file that would lead to the demise of this crew if they don't cough up the three million dollars I'm asking for. There are only two copies of the information. One folder I'm keeping for myself and the other I want you to keep safe. If anything happens to me, turn the case in to authorities," Jamal concluded.

"Whew! This is serious. So what are you going to do about your job?" Egypt asked.

"I've already quit the force so this is like a real-life poker game because I'm all in."

"Since you put it like that, I'll be more than willing to help you, but just know I want my cut."

"Egypt, you can have half... just forgive me of the choice I made to involve you in my life."

"It will take some time, but I understand the reason for your actions now," Egypt responded.

"Cool. Well I'll catch you later. I'm going to find a bar so I can get me a drink." Jamal stood up and prepared to leave.

Egypt extended her palm. "Partners?"

"Partners," Jamal replied, shaking her hand.

"Be safe, and by the way I must say that you're still a very handsome man," Egypt remarked, finally cracking a smile.

"Thanks."

***

As Youngin' walked in the crib via the garage door entrance, he shook off the effects of the cool autumn night air, welcoming the warmth of the house. Shaun was relaxing on the couch allowing 2Pac's voice coming from the sound system to marinate in her thought process.

"What's hood, sexy?" Youngin' asked, plopping down on the couch next to her.

"Just vibin' on dat gangsta shit now," Shaun replied, taking a sip from the bottle of Alizé. Youngin' was definitely infatuated with Shaun's swagger. She had her legs propped up on the table with her toes wrapped in a pair of black, chinchilla ankle-strapped pumps while the chilled bottle of Alizé was positioned between her warm thighs. She received them earlier in the day via FedEx delivery, as well as the matching, form-fitting, waist-length coat and black chinchilla bikini she was draped in.

"Wassup, you heard from Egypt today?" Youngin' asked.

"Yeah, I hit her up earlier but da broad had a lil funny style vibe tho. I peeped it, so I told her I'll catch her later. You know I'm a gangsta to da core so not too many bitches understand da real," Shaun responded.

"You think somethin' up with her?" Youngin' asked.

"I dunno, but I got my glasses on."

"Fasho."

"But I know one thang, dis pussy in need of an oil change," Shaun said as she rose from the couch to approach Youngin', leaving the black .9 mil laying on the couch.

"You know I'm 'bout dat, with yo thick ass," Youngin' replied, palming a handful of Shaun's booty while she allowed him to taste the Alizé on her juicy lips.

"Put me on camera bae so I can watch it later 'cause dis gon' be the one and only time I wear dis outfit."

"Aight, I'm with dat!" Youngin' responded excitedly as his dick began to rise in his jeans.

"I want dat gangsta shit, so beat dis pussy up good. Fuck all dat bedroom shit. We gon' get down right here, in da kitchen, shit anywhere you take me! As matter of fact, turn ya CD on," Shaun suggested, while strutting upstairs to retrieve the small hand-held camcorder.

Chapter 37

"I ain't heard from you in months, so I know you need a favor," Boss stated, leaning against the hood of a navy Crown Victoria.

"Honestly I do, but we gon' get paid, plus I don't trust anybody else with my life but you. So will you help me?"

"Long as we ain't gotta kill nobody 'cause as you can see, I got the whole Northside of town on isolation and I ain't hurtin' for no money," Boss replied.

"I fully understand and I'm only trying to put a lil more cash in your pockets. I got a outta town nigga on my line that need to be touched. Don't worry, I'm setting everything up and when the call is made. All you have to do is show up and do what you do."

"Aight I'm with it! But listen, I don't wanna know names, just call me when da action start," Boss said before lighting a Newport cigarette.

"Alright lil daddy, just be ready."

"I'm always ready. You just be ready later tonight 'cause as good as you lookin', I wanna eat you right now on da hood of da car," Boss remarked, transfixed by her camel-toe print.

"Make sho' you bring ya A-game 'cause dis good pussy is definitely overdue."

"I always do," Boss replied.

Boss remained posted up on the hood of the car and watched Retta drive away exiting the Joe Louis Projects.

"Damn, I hope dis broad got dis shit on point 'cause I finally got a real plug on da white and I don't need no mistakes," Boss thought to himself before tossing the cigarette butt to the asphalt. He hopped in the car to survey the hood.

***

Leaving the studio, Youngin' had his swag turned up to maximum with the final track from his completed album on repeat inside the Range Rover.

"Wassup? Who dis?" Youngin' asked, turning the volume down to answer the unfamiliar number.

"Someone who is very beneficial to your existence out here in these streets."

"Nigga, how the fuck you got dis number?" Youngin' yelled.

"Listen, I ain't come all the way from Dade to waste your time. Now let's try dis again. If you want to remain a free man, it's best you meet me in the CVS Pharmacy parking lot on Magnolia Drive in ten minutes," the caller stated before instantly ending the call.

"Dis fuck nigga!" Youngin' placed the black glock on his lap and decided to see exactly what the hell was going on. When Youngin' pulled into the parking lot, he noticed a Black guy wearing a white short-sleeve polo shirt with some blue khaki shorts standing against a white Ford Taurus with the swagger of a well-trained, undercover NARC. Noticing that the guy seemed to be out of place, Youngin' pulled up beside him with the window down.

"Speak, nigga!"

"No need to. You analyze these documents and return the call in no more than three days. There's only one more file like that and if the bullshit you got on your mind is acted out, instructions have already been given to turn that into authorities. If you don't want to see the demise of your crew, do the right thing. Just because you and your father killed Detective Brown, the show don't stop! Make the call and I'll tell you what I want. Nice doing business, Mr. Young," Jamal concluded. He got in the Ford Taurus and drove off without the slightest grin. Youngin' stared at the brown folder, deciding not to break the seal until he reached home.

"Damn ain't dis some shit!" he thought to himself of the déjà vu moment. When Youngin' arrived at the house it was empty, so he decided to go inside and scan through the contents of the folder. After carefully examining the files under a scrutinized view for about thirty minutes, he hesitantly redialed the number.

"What you want?" Youngin' asked when the phone was answered on the third ring.

"You got sixty days to get me three million in cash," Jamal warned.

"Den what?"

"Everything is destroyed and I go away."

"Aight, we'll meet in sixty!" Youngin' shot back.

"I'm glad we have an understanding," Jamal responded, concluding the sarcastic comment just as Youngin' ended the call.

Youngin' sat in a bittersweet daze, momentarily plotting on a way to murk Jamal, but decided against the idea while rolling a couple Backwoods.

During the midst of Youngin's solo smoke session, Shaun entered the house via the garage, suited up in a pair of black form-fitting denim jeans, a leather bubble coat and a pair of all-black Jordan 11 sneakers.

"Where you comin' from dipped in black like dat bae?" Youngin' asked.

"Oh, I went for a ride on da black stallion, lurking for dat dumb ass bitch Rain," Shaun replied, placing her motorcycle helmet on the granite countertop.

"Just be careful 'cause we ain't in Dade and these crackas bammin' niggas up here."

"I'm always on point, but wassup wit you? Look like somethin' on ya mind," Shaun inquired.

"To be real, we really in a fucked up situation, but it's nothing we ain't used to. Sit down for a minute and lemme show you something," Youngin' demanded.

"Aight, lemme pull these clothes off and slide on something more comfortable," Shaun replied, walking into one of the many bedrooms. While Shaun rinsed the cold sweat from her body in the shower, Youngin' removed the folder from underneath the couch cushion and placed it on the table. Shaun returned wearing a grey navel-length Dynamic Duo T-shirt with red embroidery and a pair of red low-rise, ass-griping Dynamic Duo brand cotton sweatpants.

As she was attempting to have a seat, Youngin' halted her movement with a gentle hand on the hip. "Damn bae I like dat dere. When you got it done?" He was referring to a fresh tattoo.

Shaun had a mural on her body that began at her waistline and had Youngin's name wrapped in cursive letters around a gold microphone. As Youngin' continued to observe the well-done image, Shaun gently pulled her pants down just below the cup of her ass, allowing Youngin' to view the remainder of the mural, which had bumblebees buzzing around the words 'Certified Star' located on her ass cheeks.

"I got tired of searching for dat scary ass bitch, so I decided to do some exclusive shit to my body today. But wassup with dat otha shit you was talkin' 'bout?" Shaun stated, snapping Youngin' out of the transfixed state he was trapped in.

"Oh yeah, my bad bae. You just fucked me up wit ya sexy ass. But yeah, check out the contents of this folder while I fix us a drink because we gon' need it," Youngin' responded as he stood to head to the kitchen.

When Youngin' returned holding two cups of ice, a bottle of Belvedere and a pitcher of kiwi-flavored Tropicana juice, Shaun blurted out, "Damn a cracka fishing down there in alligator alley done reeled out a shoe wit dat lil nigga J.B. foot still in it!"

"Yeah and da same smoker lil homie dem used to bond da nigga outta jail willing to testify on dem if need be," Youngin' stated.

"I see dat! Dese muthafuckas got a complete history of da times I used to visit Zion in da FEDS with a picture of da confrontation I had wit Rain. Shit, dis a picture of us sitting out front of Cream house the night she got murdered! Man fuck dis shit. I don't even wanna see no more of dis," Shaun exclaimed, slamming the folder shut.

"Shit gon' be straight. Buddy only got one more copy. His bitch ass talkin' 'bout fa three million cash in sixty days he'll make it all go away. I wanna kill him, but Lord knows who got da otha copy, ya smell me."

"Yeah, shit real but I know one thang fasho, I'll die befo I go to prison. Fuck it, ain't no price on freedom!" Shaun responded.

"You already know, but dis fuck nigga ain't gonna spoil my success. Da album finally complete and should be in stores soon."

"Congratulations!" Shaun replied, raising her glass cup for a toast.

"To da Duo. I'mma call lil homie dem ova and fill dem in on everything," Youngin' remarked.

"It's gon' have to wait til later tho," Shaun stated as she fondled his dick, preparing to ease his stress.

Chapter 38

"Bae, you know dat dude that got hit up in the clubs we was in a few days ago is actually in my African-American History class? The dude got a permanent scar down the left side of his face," Makayla described, while scanning through her messages on Facebook.

"Dese college thugs gon' learn 'bout playing games wit niggas who really living like dat," Will replied, slouching on the couch as his right foot, covered in an all-grey Jordan 8 sneaker, rested atop the small wooden table.

"I hear dat. So what's up dis weekend?" Makayla asked, spinning in the computer chair.

"Well Friday, my brotha Youngin' got a show in Gainesville, then on Sunday he got a show in Jacksonville at the Silver Foxx. You and Mickey gon' roll wit us?"

"Yeah, we down fa dat bae," Makayla replied excitedly.

"Aight, just be ready to ride on Friday afternoon," Will stated. He paused for a second before continuing. "Oh yeah by the way, you and Mickey gonna take turns driving if y'all can handle dat."

"That's not a problem. I'll let her know wassup when she come from the campus."

"Fasho. Well I'mma slide to go handle somethin' wit my people dem, but I'll be back to holla at ya lata," Will replied.

"I'll be here. If not, I won't be too far getting paid," Makayla replied.

"Dats what life is all about bae." Will left out the door and walked towards the orange Cadillac CTS. As he was exiting the student housing complex, the eyes of many beautiful thirsty college girls were peering down upon him, waiting for the opportunity to satiate their taste buds with a rare pedigree.

***

Veering off the Archer Road off-ramp, the four-door Yukon truck convoy headed out to the Oaks Mall in order to show face in Gainesville before Youngin's performance in about three hours. Despite the pandemonium over the Dynamic Duo Entertainment entourage, they optioned not to have any security presence surrounding them. In the midst of the hoopla, the Block Boyz left the mall and headed to a discrete location to meet a dude named D.J. from a nearby town of Williston that formerly did business with Danny Boi before his court issues forced him into the music industry. The show was initially booked to allow this pre-arranged drug transaction to take place behind the smoke and mirrors.

"What's hood?" Solo asked, as the baldheaded, basketball player framed alpha male stepped from the interior of a smoke-grey Ford Thunderbird.

"Everythang out here in da country," DJ responded, shaking hands with the trio before continuing to speak. "But I'm a hustler of your same pedigree, so I live by principles in which time and money are at da top of the list," he continued, as he passed Will a black duffel bag with four-hundred twenty-two grand neatly wrapped in rubberbands.

"It's all here. Speed pass him the sack," Will directed. He closed the black duffel bag after scanning through the bills and noticed that DJ followed instructions.

Once DJ received the sack that contained the twenty bricks of cocaine, he stated, "I might slide to da club a lil later and pop a few bottles wit my soldiers so y'all can see how we county boys put on." DJ got in the car and prepared to go stash his illegal lifeline that would provide the lavish amenities he desired.

"Aight, well just bark at us when you ready to double up," Solo stated before they departed to rejoin their entourage that was headed to the VENUE, the local Gainesville hotspot where the performance was taking place.

Chapter 39

"Man dem hoes in Jacksonville was off glass!" Speed stated.

"Yeah dey was doing dey thang, but dis bread look a lot betta, ya smell me," Will shot back as they counted out 1.5 million dollars.

"All day." Speed chimed back smiling, enjoying the natural high the money gave him.

"Wassup, Solo?" Will asked, trying to read the expression on his partner's face.

"Bout to plug my phone into da computer to check out dese photos Avia sent me of when she was up in ATL. It's also some pics of dat broad Egypt too dat she want me to show Youngin', 'cause from da way it looks, she done crept with some off breed ass nigga," Solo replied.

After scanning through the photos, aroused by a few of Avia's exclusive shots, Solo decided to drive to Youngin's spot to show him the images of Egypt and the unknown dude.

"What's hood, lil bruh?" Youngin' asked, standing to the side, allowing Solo to step through the doorway.

"Everythang when dat money is involved, ya smell me" Solo replied.

"Already."

"Ay, where ya laptop at?" Solo asked.

"On da counter by da bar, wassup?"

"I'mma show you," Solo replied, walking towards the bar top.

Once the USB card was attached to Solo's phone, he uploaded a few of the photos, enlarged the images, then spun the Dell laptop around for Youngin' to view.

"I'll be damned!" Youngin' yelled, almost burning his lip wit the cherry of the blunt. Unaware, he was attempting to smoke it from the wrong end due to total shock.

"Yeah big bruh, dat bitch ain't shit!"

"Dat ain't what I'm trippin' on. Dats da same fuck ass police officer nigga asking fa da bread that'll keep us free."

"And dese muthafuckas all in da ATL lovey-dovey and shit. Fuck it, we gon' kill dat hoe and dat fuck nigga," Solo stated.

"Dat shit sound hood, but it must be done right tho 'cause I don't need none of us going in," Youngin' replied.

"I smell you. As a matter of fact, da homie Smiley told me if we ever needed him to bark."

"Yeah do dat, 'cause too many power moves being made fa anybody to get they hands dirty on dis matter if we able to prevent. In da meantime, I'mma get dis broad on da line and peep her vibe," Youngin' concluded as he dialed Egypt's cell number and remained calm.

***

The pineapple colored sun shined bright, despite the cool breeze permeating the afternoon as Shaun stepped out of the Clippers unisex salon with a uniquely styled wrap designed by Retta. She took a

224

deep breath, relieved to be away from the array of her hair chemical aromas, before carefully sliding her biker helmet on and riding off. Less than forty-five seconds into her journey home, Shaun spotted the exact same Range Rover that followed her weeks ago waiting in the drive-thru line of Checkers.

Allowing the Range Rover to pull away from the drive-thru window first, Shaun intercepted progress, causing the driver to slam on brakes, nearly bumping into the motorcycle. Not thinking rationally, Shaun pulled the .9 mil with an extended clip from within her coat and rapidly fired at least fifteen shots through the windshield before popping a wheelie and fleeing the scene. Shaun's getaway was completed without a trace, but within two hours, the entire episode was replaying on the local WCTV news station as Shaun watched intensely.

"Just hours ago, a brutal drive-by shooting took place right in front of Checkers on South Monroe Street, as you can see, the bullet-riddled automobile behind me. The victim is 22-year old Victor Rogers, star football player at the prestigious Florida A&M University. Authorities believe the attempted assassination was intended for his possible girlfriend, Rachelle Williams, whom the SUV belongs to. She currently has not been located. The victim is in critical condition and if anyone has any information, please call 1-800-CRIMESTOPPERS. We'll have more on this investigation tonight at 11 O'clock," the reporter stated as Shaun continued staring, raising the Hennessy bottle to her face, attempting to rid her conscience of the earlier events.

Chapter 40

"Damn, it's been years since I came through the Tallahassee city limits," Smiley stated, extending a hand to Solo.

"I appreciate you for coming on such a short notice," Solo replied, taking a seat at a secluded booth within the Applebee's restaurant located on Apalachee Parkway.

"A favor for a favor. I'll die before I break my word. Just be easy and order some food 'cause we function better on a full belly," Smiley responded, signaling for the attention of the young mixed-breed waitress.

"Yeah, you right," Solo confirmed, raising the plastic menu in his view.

"Oh by the way, call the homies and tell them to pick up the cars from the Comfort Suites Hotel parking lot down from the Governor's Square Mall," Smiley commanded, just as the waitress approached the booth. As Smiley was placing his order, Solo conducted business, informing Will and Speed of where to pick up the work while at the same time dropping off the funds.

While eating, the two discussed everything from sports to women, having a mutual understanding that the walls were possibly listening, so proper discretion of words was a must.

"Listen, I'll be in town, so holla at me when da rat come fa da cheese," Smiley stated, arising from the table.

"Say no more," Solo replied, shaking hands with Smiley before walking outside and lighting a Black & Mild, blowing the smoke cloud into the sky.

***

"Damn chick, where you been hiding at?" Jamilah asked.

"Just been laying low like a bad bitch supposed to," Shaun replied, having a seat at a table located within the interior of the exact same Zaxby's restaurant where they met months prior.

"Dats wassup. Of course we called you here 'cause me and Shay gon' slide up to ATL in two days. Yeah da spider senses kicked in 'bout a month ago when we spotted a potential money bag. Bored as hell and a few hours later, we were led to his spot in da 'A'. After doing homework, we a sent a thank-you prayer up to da gods for blessin' us with the gift for the keen scent for da money," Jamilah explained, smiling.

"Just lace me up on da way there because I need a vacation from dis country ass town anyway," Shaun complained.

Relinquishing a light chuckle, Shay stated, "If anybody understand you we do, but uh, Shaun, look like you got a fan dat work here." She pointed to the guy wearing a light blue collar shirt, possibly signifying the position of being the shift manger. Shaun spun around exclaiming, "Oh hell naw! Is it me or does dis nigga really look like a possum wit golds?" Shay and Jamilah laughed uncontrollably.

"But shit, I'mma finesse dis mark for some free food just for the hell of it," Shaun concluded, walking to the front counter seeking a good laugh.

Chapter 41

Intricately positioned inside the Blue Flame Strip Club, Shaun and Jamilah camouflaged themselves as two patrons appeased by the naked hustle. They ordered a couple bottles of Moët as various women frequently entertained them, and out of respect for the grind, two ladies tossed the desired American currency in the direction of the beautiful Georgia peaches. In the midst of the glitz and glam, the two ladies remained focused on the ultimate mission at hand while Shay waited outside, secluded within the interior of the black-on-black Porsche Carrera. On this particular night, Cash decided to enjoy the booty popping bonanza from the V.I.P. area of the club instead of the back office as usual. Cash was actually co-owner of the club with his longtime associate.

Many of the women dancing were slaves to Cash's mental manipulation, as a few others were reminiscent of indentured servants working for their freedom. At first glance, one couldn't determine Cash's wealth, but his longevity in the game spoke for itself as he was one of the remaining players left from the mid-80s.

After vibing for about two hours, Cash scooped up his monthly profits and exited out the back door. Normally, Cash would remain in the establishment longer, but he was enticed by the payout offered by his somewhat new, extra-curricular clientele. Shay alerted Jamilah that the target was creeping out the back door and she and Shaun left out immediately, hopping in the adjacent black-on-black Carrera that they arrived in. The two-car hit squad followed Cash as he traveled down Godby Road and merged onto I-75 southbound, arriving at a hotel near Southlake Mall.

Cash never exited the vehicle; he kept the car running as a young lady came out the side door of the Hampton Inn carrying a Christian Dior duffel bag. Shaun couldn't believe her eyes as Rain hopped in the passenger seat of Cash's car. Despite her anger, Shaun humbled her emotions for the benefit of the lick they were on. The ladies continued to follow Cash to a secluded home in the suburban area of Stockbridge on a street titled Buckington Place, where his storybook night was soon to turn tragic.

As the garage door was winding down behind the BMW, Jamilah covered in her all-black cat suit rolled underneath and crouched behind the car unnoticed.

"You done drove dis far to get dis good dick, so I'mma make sho' you get ya money worth," Cash stated, stepping out of the car, unaware that Rain fled Tallahassee after her attempted assassination.

Once Cash deactivated the Brinks home alarm system, he farted and pissed on himself at the same time as Jamilah whispered, "If you scream, both of y'all gon' be tomorrow's sushi buffet dinner," while aiming an all-black Russian AK-47 pistol grip.

"I'll give you whatever you want, just don't kill me," Cash cried nervously, with his palms up as piss trailed down his legs.

"First of all, go inside and open the front door. Don't try no funny shit 'cause my finger already twitchin',” Jamilah warned, walking them to the front door with the barrel pointed directly at them. Shaun walked in barrel first, never uttering a word, strictly about the business at hand.

“Let's make this transaction quick with less blood as possible. Open ya safe for us and we'll be gone before you know what happened,” Jamilah bargained, as Cash nodded his head in agreement.

Cash had numerous places where he stashed his savings and this particular home held a little over two million neatly stacked. He didn't hesitate relinquishing because he considered his life more valuable. Within five minutes, Jamilah had the bags loaded up as Shaun continued to hold them at gunpoint.

“It was nice to take ya bread without having to kill you,” Jamilah said in a taunting demeanor while backing out the door with the barrel of the assault rifle still aimed.

“Cash, get yaself checked out ‘cause dis bitch got AIDS!” Shaun exclaimed, causing Rain to cringe upon voice recognition, but she had no chance to respond as her fragile nose was broken again with the butt of the pistol grip. Cash let out a loud exhale when the robber's fled the vicinity before speaking.

“Come on upstairs and let me get you cleaned up. If I find out you had anything to do with this, ya fasho gon' be dead, and trust me you can try to run, but I got killers on my payroll dat will hunt you till you drop. By the way, you betta not be done gave me dat shit either!” Rain just remained silent on how she would escape and hunt Shaun down, who she was for certain was one of the masked robbers.

The three women escaped down Interstate 75, never relinquishing momentum on the gas pedal until they merged onto highway 319 coming through the Thomasville, Georgia, city limits. The payout was adequate and they began to relax as they approached the homefront.

Chapter 42

"If shit don't look right in there, you already know what to do. I'mma keep da car running," Youngin' stated. Shaun stepped out the driver side of the Porsche Cayenne carrying a large black bag from Express, along with a dark brown paper bag from JCPenney. Shaun headed directly to the food court and took a seat in front of Sbarro's Pizza while awaiting Jamal's transporter to arrive. Speed sat nearby eating a burger from Wendy's with the second portion of the payment within a Dillard's bag and a Finish Line bag with two shoe boxes filled with money.

When Shaun noticed Egypt approaching, she was in total shock at her audacity. Despite her anger, Shaun completed the task at hand while Speed transferred the money to Jamal at the same time following suit. Unbeknownst to Jamal and Egypt, there were two sets of eyes upon them that could follow and never raise any suspicion. Watching the event unfold from in front of the Smoothie Café, Kim and Mary were draped in all white businesswoman-like pantsuits prepared to fulfill the mission Smiley sent them on.

"Everythang hood?" Youngin' asked as Shaun sat back in the automobile.

"Yeah, shit straight but dat disloyal bitch was da one who picked up da drop from lil bruh," Shaun replied with a look of disgust on her face.

"I figured dat already, but dem stupid muthafuckas won't get far because dem white ninja assassins on dey ass without a sound, ya smell me."

"Yeah, I'm smellin' you but I need some dick and fa you to smell dis pussy right now to ease my stress level so I'm finna head to the house," Shaun remarked as Youngin' passed her the remnants of the blunt he was smoking.

"We ain't even got to go home, just lean da seat all the way back," Youngin' replied as Shaun did as told.

Youngin' helped Shaun slide out of her jeans as he squatted down between her legs that were propped up on the dashboard. He didn't remove the lime-green T-backs; instead Youngin' used two fingers to hold the fabric covering her pussy to the side. The thrill of getting her pussy licked while watching people walk in and out the mall aroused her deeply because it was as if she was putting on a show for the audience. Youngin's tongue operated upon her clit as if there was a battery pack stored within with unlimited power, which caused Shaun to cum uncontrollably three times in a fifteen-minute span. The leather seats were reminiscent of a set of freshly waxed Armor All tires due to all of Shaun's orgasmic juices that continued to flow. Youngin' raised his head up and kissed Shaun passionately, allowing her to taste her own juices, and she was more than willing to succumb to the gesture.

"Alright let's go to da house and you drive," Youngin' stated.

"Yes daddy, but I ain't puttin' my pants on tho. I want you to play wit dis pussy while I drive," Shaun teased as Youngin' unlocked Pandora's Box. She was willing to do anything to please him.

"Aight, let's ride and don't wreck out babygirl," Youngin' stated, sliding two fingers in her pussy and then inserting those same two fingers in her mouth.

"Oooh daddy, I love you!" Shaun shouted out in pleasure, feenin' for more.

***

"I told you I was done wit dat lifestyle, dats why I moved back to Florida," Avia said over the phone in an agitated manner.

"I understand that clearly, but you da one who said that if I ever needed a favor to call. Don't forget you got da magazine off da ground doin' dis same type of work on my face. So technically, you owe me!"

"Whatever. Dis da last time tho and after dis, never call me again on dis type of shit," Avia responded.

"Aight, no problem. Lashaunda Scott is da name from Miami, but possibly located in Tallahassee running with a rap label crew called Dynamic Duo. When I see a finger, you got your money."

"Roger dat!" Avia responded.

After ending the call, contemplating for a while, Avia stated aloud to herself, "Hell naw, I fucks with Shaun and da fam 'cause they keep it real. What I do kno is dat I'mma kill dat fuck boy tho 'cause he think I forgot how he tried me!"

Chapter 43

"What they do?" Youngin' asked, answering the cellphone call.

"Everything you on, sexy. But uh, where you at now? I wanna see you, or should I say I need you, if you know what I mean," Retta stated seductively.

"Yeah, I know exactly what you mean," Youngin' replied, pausing consciously, debating whether or not to invite her to the spot while Shaun was out with Shay and Jamilah.

"As a matter of fact, slide to my house ova here in Southwood," Youngin' continued, deciding that Retta was worthy enough to see the spot.

"Alright daddy, I'm on my way," Retta responded, jotting directions down on a scrap of Winn-Dixie receipt paper. Youngin' ended the call then went into the kitchen to mix a Blue Alizé and Belvedere margarita to help warm Retta's body from the Florida Panhandle winter chill. In the meantime, he performed his ritual of smoking a phat blunt, preparing to give Retta a Dade-County dickdown.

***

"So how da streets been treating you?" Danny Boi asked. At this very moment he had the two-door 2009 Chevy Monte Carlo backed into a parking space deep within the trenches of Joe Louis Projects.

"You already kno dat. Besides you, da streets da only family dat loved me so I'm good. I got da city on smash ever since ya lil partner dem been blessin a G," Boss replied, reaching for the blunt Danny Boi passed.

"I feel dat. Well since you eating like dat now, come represent wit da real tonight at my dawg Youngin' birthday bash. We got da School Boyz on da ones and twos holdin' us down so you know it's gonna be live," Danny Boi stated.

"Shit, I'm feelin dat! Hold on for a second, lemme answer dis call," Boss replied while reaching for his phone. Within a twenty second interval, Boss had memorized every word the caller spoke before tapping the end key.

"Wassup?" Danny Boi asked, noticing the quizzical look on Boss's face.

"Man to be honest, I got a major lick dat dis broad Retta got set up right now. I hate to ask, but will you drive me ova there and watch my back? Da shit sweet so I'll be out in three minutes," Boss guaranteed.

"I ain't hurtin' fa no bread, plus you know I'm on dis industry shit right now. But just to make sho' you don't catch no life sentence, I'mma roll. Don't ever do dis shit again and never question my loyalty to you," Danny Boi remarked while inwardly attempting to remember where he heard the name Retta mentioned.

When Danny Boi pulled near the house that Boss directed him to, he shouted, "Oh hell naw! Dis my nigga Youngin' crib!"

"Listen D-Boi, I didn't know who I was comin' to hit 'cause I asked dat she didn't mention names, but now dat I know wassup, I ain't wit it," Boss responded.

"Shit I hope not, 'cause da lil niggas you been copping work from is his fam and I believe all my niggas 'bout dat life," Danny Boi stated, calling Youngin' to alert him of his presence outside.

Once Danny Boi ended the call, he stated, "Come on, we gon' go inside."

"How 'bout dat! Da baddest bitches in da game showed up right on time fa da party." He noticed Shay, Shaun, and Jamilah as they arrived in the driveway. They all walked in the home together as Youngin' sat at the granite countertop bar shirtless with his Dynamic Duo chain draped around his neck, sipping margaritas.

"What they do? Wassup, y'all having a pre-birthday party fa da boy in here?" Youngin' asked, greeting everyone with much positive enthusiasm.

Retta peeped the vibe and stated, "Well this seems to be a family affair so I'll catch y'all at the birthday bash tonight." She attempted to make her way out the front door.

"I hate to bust ya bubble, but you won't be leaving dat easily," Danny Boi remarked, blocking her path.

"Look, I don't want any trouble," Retta replied.

"Apparently you did, trying to have my partner Youngin' robbed!" Danny Boi exclaimed, causing everyone in the room to instantly switch into a war-like mindstate.

"You stupid bitch!" Shaun shouted, hitting Retta in the back of the head with the Belvedere bottle that was on the counter, but it didn't break upon contact. Retta fell to the floor holding the back of her head sobbing.

"I didn't know what else to do because I need to get my sister back."

"You can tell dat to your maker when you meet him 'cause dats where yo ass is goin'!" Shaun exclaimed, gripping a handful of her hair, preparing to drag her out to the trunk to dump her soon-to-be dead body some place. Boss, unable to control his emotions, pulled out two black glocks as if he was a seasoned gunslinger from a western movie.

"Listen, I don't wanna kill nobody, but I ain't gonna let y'all kill her either, so just let her go and everything with be aight."

"Fool, you kno you trippin', right?" Danny Boi remarked.

"Man, fuck all dat! Retta go start da car, I'm right behind you," Boss retorted as Retta was walking in his direction. Once Retta was safely outside, Boss backed out the doorway.

"I don't want no problems, so if y'all don't start nothin', it won't be nothin'." He made it to the passenger seat of Retta's vehicle, finally breathing easily as they rode away. Boss knew the fire was ignited so he wisely made preparations for him and Retta to leave town as soon as possible. Inside the home, Youngin' kept everyone at bay.

"It's hood, we'll catch 'em. But fa now, I just wanna enjoy my birthday wit da Duo." Danny Boi agreed for the present moment, but inwardly vowed to show Boss that he was still the king of the capital city, 850 area code.

Chapter 44

After moments of reading through the Rolling Stone Magazine, Shaun raised her head and stated, "Damn bae, Billboard 100 ranked Flo Motion number 55 on da charts!" Youngin' remained silent while staring down at the twentieth floor window at the DoubleTree Hotel in downtown Tallahassee.

Breaking his silence, he replied in a raspy tone, "You know I feel like a tiger caged in a 200 because dis industry shit just ain't my natural environment. Don't get me wrong, dats a big accomplishment for my first single, but lately I been straight off dis country ass town."

"So what you wanna do?" Shaun asked, propping her feet up on the plush footstool, simultaneously turning on the television.

"My mind telling me to get back to da bottom, but I don't wanna move too fast and it be a bad move," Youngin' replied, taking a seat next to Shaun.

"I say we get back to da bottom of da clip and get back on our square because shit up this way is for the birds, plus these crackas racist ass fuck!"

"Speaking of racist, turn da volume up. Dis dat Troy Davis execution some of our Black leaders been tryin' to stop," Youngin' stated, directing his attention to the CNN broadcast.

"Dem pussy ass crackas ain't stop lynching us yet. We need to get back on dat Black Panther movement 'cause dese crackas understand nothing but pressure!" Shaun exclaimed, expressing her dislike for ignorant Caucasians manipulating the legal system.

"I'm definitely on dat, but we need all our people to stand up and fight for a righteous cause like dem Zoes did in Haiti in 1804. You can't be afraid to shed or lose some blood, ya smell me," Youngin' remarked as a lone tear fell from his eye while the execution was displayed on live TV.

"I was born wit dat revolutionary shit in my veins, but fuck it, put a wet towel under da door so I can fire dis up," Shaun responded, holding a blunt between her index and forefinger.

***

Closing his Nextel i730 flip cellphone, Boss nearly buckled over while standing in the checkout line of the Wal-Mart with Retta locked in Bainbridge, Georgia. The look on his face held the expression of disaster, but he maintained his composure until he and Retta returned to the hotel they chose to lay low at for a while.

"Ay Retta, I gotta leave you here for a few 'cause some shit went down and I gotta ride 'bout mine," Boss stated.

"What happened?"

"My auntie Michelle just called me while I was in Wal-Mart and informed me my momma, baby momma and my four-year old son was just found floating butt-naked on S. Georgia Island Beach," Boss replied, nearly breaking down in tears.

"Damn, why did they involve them?" Retta asked, beginning to cry uncontrollably.

242

"Just to get to me. There's no rules in war, so I can't cry over the repercussions. What I will do is ride so just hang out here til I get back. You'll be safe," Boss promised.

"I'm scared as fuck!" Retta exclaimed.

"Just hold dis down, you'll be alright. I gotta go," Boss replied, passing her a .22 mil and a box of bullets before walking out the hotel room. Unbeknownst to Boss, Danny Boi had already issued the hit throughout the city. The very moment he broke the barrier of the Leon County city limits, his head had to stay on a swivel.

At the same time, Retta's well-being was in jeopardy because Shay and Jamilah used their resources to track down Retta's last known credit card transaction that directed them to the Comfort Suites in Bainbridge, Georgia. Retta, already anticipating the worst, waited on Boss to leave before calling a taxicab. She was destined for the nearest rental car agency, preparing to jump the state lines once more in an attempt to preserve her life.

Chapter 45

"Moments ago, a brutal altercation took place right here at the location of 300 West Tharpe Street in Tallahassee. An African-American male known by the alias name Boss, born T.J Henderson, believed to be the originator of the shooting, has been pronounced dead on the scene. A second male, known to be a local hip-hop star by the name of Danny Boi has been rushed to Tallahassee Memorial Hospital with critical injuries. His status is unknown at the present moment. A third man, known to be C.E.O of the entertainment label Dynamic Duo, Lyric Jones, is presently identified as one of the victims and possible shooter in the line of self-defense in the death of T.J Henderson. Authorities have yet to release any further information but are asking for any possible witnesses to come forward." The WCTV reporter broke this news via the television as Shaun sat stunned, with her mouth agape as Youngin' walked into the hotel room.

"Shaun wassup, why you looking like dat?" Youngin' asked, plopping down on the couch next to her.

Trying her best to control her emotions, Shaun replied, "Danny Boi just got shot in front of the studio."

"Damn I just left him and Lyric there," Youngin' replied, attempting to dial Lyric's cellphone number.

"Yeah, he supposedly killed da dude Boss who more than likely shot bruh," Shaun assumed, gliding her fingernails backwards through her hair in a frustrated manner. Once Youngin' ended the phone call conversation, Shaun continued. "Lyric just left the interrogation headquarters on 7th Avenue as dem crackas pulled the tape from the cameras outside the studio, which possibly saved him from further speculations. Plus the firearm he used was licensed and registered under his name. He headed over to the hospital right now. I told him I'll meet him there. You ridin'?"

"Yeah I'm ridin', give me a few minutes to tighten myself up," Shaun replied, walking towards the bathroom.

Thirty minutes later, they entered the hospital double doors and were greeted by a sea of crying women and stern-faced gangsters who all prayed silently that Danny Boi would escape death. Once the green light was issued by Lyric, the nurses escorted Youngin' and Shaun to another waiting area where few family members were allowed to wait. For a total of three days that seemed prolonged more than others, Danny Boi remained in a coma with a bullet wound to the side of his neck and two bullet wounds in the chest, inches away from a vital organ. Doctors were shocked that he was even fighting for his life due to the severity of the injuries. On the third day, Danny Boi finally opened his eyes. He was unable to speak, so he simply nodded to the nurses, signifying that he was back from the dead.

The news spread throughout the hospital rapidly as everyone finally began crying tears of relief, especially his mom and sister who had been fasting and praying for three days straight. Despite surviving, Danny Boi's career as a hip-hop melodist was possibly over due to the wound near his vocal box.

***

"Bitches wanna play wit my fetti, huh? No pressure though, I'm coming to see 'bout ya," Cash stated to himself, hanging up the phone attempting to reach Retta.

Counting his journey on Highway 319 South, Cash traveled through Thomasville city limits, soon to be arriving in Tallahassee to meet up with an associate of his. Following the directions he was given led him directly to the desired location of the Collegiate Inn Motel on Tennessee Street and the intersection of Ocala Road in Tallahassee.

"I'm out here," Cash announced as his phone rested in his lap on speakerphone.

"Come to room 217. I'm unlocking the door now."

When Cash stepped across the threshold of the doorway, Avia was coolin' like a window air conditioner, draped in some black satin fabric panties and bra set with gold trimming.

"Lock da door behind you," Avia demanded before taking a seat on the couch.

"Wassup wit dat bizz, you handled it, right?" Cash asked.

"As always. Here's a few pictures of what your jackers looked like before they met their maker."

Avia slid a couple photos of the ladies on the table just to satisfy Cash's curiosity.

"Damn, ain't dat a bitch 'cause dese same broads were in da club dat night!"

"Yeah, yeah fuck all dat emotional shit. Let me show you da finger. You got my bread?" Avia asked, rising to her feet over to the small refrigerator, as if she really had something within.

Instead, she poured herself a stiff shot of V.S.O.P cognac while discreetly grabbing her .9 mil silencer pistol. In the midst of Avia pouring a drink, Cash pulled out a personal stash of cocaine and proceeded to toot the powder through his nostrils. When Cash raised his head, Avia stood before him with a gun raised, causing him to resemble a deer blinded by the headlights.

"Pussyclot bwoi, mi never forget wat you dun to me dere!" Avia exclaimed as her patoís accent surfaced, unintentionally. Her anger rose, causing her to fire three rounds through his thick skull, along with three more to his chest.

For the next forty-five minutes, Avia meticulously revamped all the steps that she strategically walked throughout the room using Johnson & Johnson brand baby wipes to erase any possible trace that she was there. The room was rented under a phony identification so she had no worries. Knowing the way Cash moved about throughout the land with plenty money with him, Avia decided to check the vehicle for extra compensation.

Upon popping the trunk, Avia exclaimed in a barely audible tone, "What the fuck!" She noticed two nude women gagged and hogtied. Blinded by the light, the women began squirming at the thought of their demise.

"Please don't kill me," the first young Black woman named Shamiya, Retta's sister, stated with fear stricken throughout her naked body as Avia removed the gag. After removing the other woman's muzzle, Avia heard her speak.

"Yeah, please, please don't kill us." Rain whimpered out for sympathy.

"Listen, I'm going to untie your hands, but the rest is on you. I'm also leaving the keys to this car, but if y'all have it more than one day, it could bring trouble," Avia filled them in, calming the frightened women before exiting the scene, unnoticed by anyone. If she was spotted, the wig along with the other phony pieces would conceal her true image.

Unbeknownst to her faculty of reasoning, Avia was placing two of the most dangerous women, health-wise, back in motion throughout the state of Florida. Since Shamiya shared a common bond with Rain after being held captive together, Rain's influence over Shamiya's decision to follow her to Miami wouldn't be hard.

Within the car, near the vicinity of the crime, Avia spoke over the phone via speaker. "Lo baby wassup, you busy?"

"Not really, where you at?" Solo replied with a return question.

"Headed to the mall. I need you to meet me there on da side by da Ruby Tuesday in five minutes," Avia informed, dipping through the college town traffic.

"Aight, I got you," Solo replied, moving hastily, comprehending the tension in her voice.

Approximately three minutes later, Avia was parking an unwanted automobile that was purchased under the table for a minute amount of cash on the adjacent side of the mall near JCPenney. After parking the car, Avia finally peeled off the gloves she was wearing and stuffed them in her oversized handbag while gracefully strutting through the interior of the mall. Avia made a brief stop in the ladies' room, quickly peeling off the extra amenities and storing them in the handbag as well before exiting the mall on the opposite side, just as Solo was pulling up.

"What up boo, everything hood?" Solo asked as Avia sat on the passenger side.

"Yeah, just put da car in motion and I'll tell you," Avia replied, reclining the seat and inhaling deeply. She prepared to lace Solo's mental with everything that transpired, as well as little known facts about her identity.

Chapter 46

Less than three months later, upon special request, Youngin' sat aboard a first-class flight to Puerto Rico to have a meeting with some special people. When he arrived at the terminal, he was met by a very militant man with a freshly cut fade, who was chauffeuring him to the desired destination. During the entire trip to the secluded location, the Latin driver never uttered a word while navigating the all-black bulletproof 760Li BMW vehicle. Stepping out of the interior of the automobile within the confines of the private property on the island, Youngin' was greeted by a half-naked, yellow tanned Latin mamí.

"Qué hola papí?" She asked as she handed him an exclusive Cohiba cigar.

"No tranquilo," Youngin' replied.

"Señor Smiley te esta esperado," the beautiful island woman continued stating in Spanish dialect.

"Tambien," Youngin' replied, thankful that he paid attention in Spanish class during the times he did attend high school.

After being led to an oversized backyard, Smiley waited atop a palm tree thatched pool chair, sipping a piña colada mixed with Absolut Vodka.

"Have a seat," Smiley urged. Once Youngin' sat down, Smiley extended a handshake.

"How was the trip?"

"Cozy. Got treated like royalty," Youngin' replied.

"That's good. Well, yes, Mr. Youngin', we both are men with little time to waste, so I'll get down to business. Of course that package you desperately wanted was scooped up in the Virgin Islands. Instead of destroying valuable goods, I brought the rare treasures here to this island. Would you like to see them?" Smiley asked.

"Yes," Youngin' responded with vengeance spelled out on his face.

"Very well, follow me," Smiley ordered, standing and smoothing out the wrinkles in his white, linen shorts, leading the way across the ceramic-glassed pool deck. His white Prada loafers lightly clacked rhythmically on the surface. As they approached a door that concealed the confines of a room located five feet underground, there was a husky Puerto Rican dude guarding the entrance. When Youngin' entered the room, the feeling of hitting the jackpot twice at the Vegas Bellagio Hotel permeated through his pores as he saw Jamal and Egypt strapped down in two separate wooden chairs.

"Was da money really worth your life?" Youngin' directed his comment at both of them, not really seeking a response.

"Youngin', please don't kill me. I'm sorry." Egypt whimpered for her life to be spared.

"You definitely sorry for even attempting to befriend dis chump, but my time is precious and my words for y'all left with my money," Youngin' stated before using the pistol Smiley prepared for him. He killed them both, while staring into their eyes.

Youngin' left the room with a cold look as his heart inwardly shed a tear because he had a thing for Egypt. But the principles of love, respect and loyalty, which he stood for as a man of integrity, allowed him to continue on without an outward show of emotion. The mutual respect he and Smiley shared was understood and didn't need to be explained, as money was still their top priority. Smiley would soon be delivering his products to the Block Boyz as Youngin' also had a grind to get back to himself.

Three hours later, Youngin' was once again in the backseat of the 760Li, heading to the airport for the flight back to the states. As Youngin' was about to step out the car, the driver who was Puerto Rico's last standing kingpin in disguise spoke.

"Señor, if it's not too much to ask, I need a favor of you. My brother, Paco, was killed in Miami about a year ago and the killer is still unknown. My name is Wisdom and if you ever hear the slightest rumor, contact me please." He handed him a black and gold business card.

"No problem," Youngin' answered, before stepping out the car.

When Youngin' returned to the Fort Lauderdale Airport terminal, tipsy due to the first-class airline liquor, Shaun was waiting out front in the Porsche Cayenne, ready to take off.

"Everything go aight?" Shaun asked as Youngin' closed the passenger door.

"As always," Youngin' replied, pausing for a second to wind down the window and stick his head out to get reacquainted with the intoxicating South Florida atmosphere.

"You got dat, bae?" Youngin' asked, referring to the South Florida grown kryptonite weed he needed to clear his mind.

"Yeah, it's in the glove compartment," Shaun responded while merging onto Interstate 595 westbound, using the radio remote to crank the pioneer system to the max as "Mr. Wrong" by Mary J. Blige featuring Drake began to tingle her soul down to the original cell. She was definitely feeling the vibe now that Youngin' was back.

***

"Big money!" Solo shouted, tossing the two red dice towards the wall on the side of the corner store. In the midst of the crap game were six other Jamaican hustlers that had money gripped in the palms of their hands as miscellaneous cash was spread abroad on the pavement while bets were being placed on the next roll. Once the entire crew dispersed from Tallahassee, per Avia's request, Solo switched up the location of the Block Boyz to Deepside Lauderhill where her family hustled. At the current moment, Solo was at the store on 55th Avenue while Speed and Will were strategically positioned on 56th Avenue, holding down the trap in shifts as hustlers from Lake Worth down to the Florida Keys shopped with them. The motion on their money machine never relinquished forward progress.

"Bet back bredren," a slim-built Rastafarian wearing a black silk wife beater stated, dropping two stacks on the pavement.

"No pressure badmon," Solo replied as his cellphone rang at the same time.

"Pardon mi soul bredren," Solo remarked, stepping aside to answer the caller.

"What's hood, big bruh?" Solo asked enthusiastically.

"Fivin'. Ay, but y'all boys presence would be a blessin' tonight at Chili Peppers fa my show. Everybody gon' be out," Youngin' stated, referring to a club near Las Olas Boulevard in downtown Fort Lauderdale.

"Bruh for you, Danny Boi, Lyric and da rest of da fam, I'm all in at all times. We gon' be in da building, ain't no pressure," Solo replied.

"Aight, I'll see y'all boys in a lil bit," Youngin' confirmed, ending the call.

Solo spun around and dropped seven-hundred dollars in the main bank of the dice game.

"Shottas, I gotta blaze, but I'll holla later." He walked off to a 1993 Buick with five percent tint that he slid around town in as his newfound wealth remained undetectable. Solo understood that tonight would be the first time since Danny Boi's shooting that he'd be making an appearance in the limelight. Prior to this, Youngin' cancelled many tour dates due to the incident, but tonight, everyone in the Dynamic Duo family would be showing support, representing for the real. So, his foresight told him it would be a night for the paparazzi to capture star-studded history and he and the Block Boyz were going to put on.